shopping Lessons

by Peller Marion

Artemis Arts Library
San Francisco
2004

Shopping Lessons

Artemis Arts Library USA
San Francisco, Ca. 94111
www.Artemisartslibrary.com

First Edition

Printed in the United States of America

Designed by Laurence Brauer; Wordsworth

Cover painting by Peller Marion. Mixed media. 2004.

ISBN O-9746927-5-1

To my father and mother

1

"You're gonna love this guy. Real talent." Sharon was effusive over the phone. We both were on a talent scout search, and we used this type of girl code for the manhunt. At thirty-six, I was feeling a lot of pressure to find a man to marry.

"Do you think he's Mr. Right?" I asked. She was my closest friend and former roommate, several years older than I. Sometimes it felt like she was my big sister. We had driven across country and I introduced her to California. She quit her teaching job at Amherst and moved to the Bay Area shortly afterwards.

"He *could* be Mr. Right," she offered.

When I saw David at the intermission at the professional conference, I knew exactly what she meant. He was very tall and broad-shouldered. Jewish men didn't usually come this way.

I was entranced with how he was like a gigantic eucalyptus tree, and how the planes of his face were open and angular. His light blue eyes were like agate marbles. And that head of curly dark brown hair — fine like a baby's — made me want to pull him to my breast and suckle him, or take him to bed and fuck his brains out. He had that cold-on-the-outside, warm-on-the-inside feel to him. Sharon had described it as "fire and ice." And now I saw what she meant. There was a Nick Nolte don't-mess-with-me way about him. I could see the outline of his tee shirt underneath his soft white sweater, and could smell him close to his skin.

After brief introductions, Sharon smiled smugly and receded to the sidelines. She had scored and she knew it.

"Are you going to the party tonight, after this?" I asked him.

"Oh, the one at Mike's house?"

"Yes."

"I didn't think I would go, but now I think I might. Will you be there?" He smiled at me.

God, I loved how those crooked front teeth formed that smile. It made my heart pound. He reminded me of Ollie from "Kukla, Fran and Ollie," a kids' television show with a wide-eyed boy puppet, Kukla a dragon puppet and a woman, Fran.

Suddenly the lights dimmed, signaling us that the second half of the program was about to start. We all started moving. In the crush, I mouthed, yes and smiled — a big, broad, inviting smile. He returned to his seat in the front of the auditorium, and I went back to sit with Sharon.

That night I found Mike's house in a run-down section of the city. Everyone was crowding into the tiny kitchen. Only Sharon and David were in the dining room doing a kind of dirty dancing, not really touching, but swaying two inches apart facing and following each other with their eyes to the soft seduction of Barry White. She barely said hello to me as I greeted her. She had his cowboy hat on her head, which gave off a very territorial message. He didn't even look my way.

My heart sank. What the hell was she doing taking over my guy? I thought, as I walked back into the kitchen. I was pissed at her.

It was beginning to feel like one of those long nights that are the worst part of being single — working very hard at "trying to have fun."

Someone changed the music to *Saturday Night Fever.* The tempo picked up, and a pimply guy named Dwayne asked me to dance. He took me in his arms. My spiked heels beat out the rhythm. My body, in a black leotard top and circle skirt, responded effortlessly to his lead. Miraculously, he transformed into John Travolta and I into Karen Lynn Gorney, as we sidestepped, twisted and twirled around the dance floor. A hush fell over the dancers as they moved to give us a wide berth. For several minutes, our brilliance of timing, pacing and dipping permeated the room. All the years of those temple dance classes had paid off!

Surely now David would notice me and want to dance with me.

"Way to go, girl!" Sharon whispered in my ear as the music ended. David was at her side. Everyone edged back into the kitchen. David resumed dancing with Sharon. He didn't even look my way. I left the party as soon as I could.

In the next several weeks, I avoided Sharon and busied myself with searching for a job, so when David called one day out of the blue, I was taken aback. I had assumed I didn't have a chance. I rationalized that this was the life of a single person — the good, the bad and the ugly of it.

Mom never suffered from this, according to her ebullient description of the moonlit night in 1936 when she met and danced with Dad at the lake in her yellow chiffon dress, while his band played her special requests.

"Hi, this is David. I met you several weeks ago at a conference. Your friend Sharon introduced us. Do you remember me?"

I snapped back, "Yes, of course. What took you so long to call?"

He laughed. "Well, I've been very busy with my work. Would you like to go out for brunch tomorrow?"

He went on to say that he was a consultant, and that he had been called out of town on some crisis. I wondered if it was to solve the Israeli crisis, maybe to help Golda Meir, but I kept my mouth shut.

Mom and Dad were married within three months of meeting each other, and they gave birth to my brother Harry exactly ten months later. "Dad was my Prince Charming. He always greeted me with a yellow rose during our courtship," Mom reminded me.

Little did I know that David and I were just beginning our long exploration into ambivalence — punctuated by short periods of intimacy and commitment — that would last for the next six years.

"Your dad was the specimen of good health when I met him," Mom told me. We were looking at the photo album marked "The Courtship Years." Dad stood flexing the muscles of his arms. I had to nod in agreement that Dad looked like a real Jewish Charles Atlas.

David had lost his hearing in his right ear just before he met me. It happened on a long plane ride home from a consulting job. They couldn't stop the viral infection in time.

The other difficulty was that he was seeing several other women, and possibly sleeping with them.

We had been seeing each other for a month when the holidays loomed ahead. That's prime time for single people, and a real dilemma for the newly dating. "What are you planning to do for Thanksgiving?" I asked him two Saturday nights before that special Thursday.

"I've been invited to a workshop on how to spend Thanksgiving," he said, then paused, "with Lana."

I balked. My mouth opened wide for the dramatic effect. "You need to take lessons in how to spend Thanksgiving? An adult like you, with a very important job?"

"Well, how would you spend Thanksgiving?" he asked slyly.

"I'd take my little Fiat Spyder convertible, pack our stuff and drive down the coast to Santa Barbara. We'd check into a hotel, walk on the beach, order room service and ride bicycles." I was being spontaneous, not having thought a moment about this, except that I wanted to be with him. So I made it up as I went along.

"Sounds like a plan!" he said excitedly.

I had never heard specifics of Lana, but I knew I had scored, and that's all that mattered to me.

Mom told me that she had never slept with anyone before Dad. She was a twenty-eight-year-old virgin when they married. David and I made love shortly after the second date. I was so turned on by him that I would have slept with him on the first date, but even I knew that was bad etiquette.

David seduced me, or maybe I seduced him. His apartment was set up like a real hustling den: frozen quiches stacked in the freezer, several bottles of champagne hanging off the refrigerator door, chilled tins of caviar and smoked oysters on the second shelf, and a few boxes of English crackers sitting on otherwise empty cupboard shelves. He was no stranger to this routine, but then again, I wasn't either.

We hadn't gotten any farther than the champagne when we found ourselves on his king-size mattress on the floor in his otherwise empty bedroom. At three o'clock in the morning, after some aerobic sex, we had worked up an appetite for the oysters, crackers and cheese, which we ate naked, standing at the kitchen counter.

I knew that I was reeling in a big, live, restless one, but I loved what I had seen so far: his complexity, the way his face would soften, and how gentle he was with me. He talked about wanting to do something big in the world, something creative, where people would be helped and valued in corporations.

He apologized for waiting two weeks to call me. He said he had been intimidated by my dance performance, and was afraid to call. That endeared him to me even more.

Mom told me that I shouldn't get involved with someone with a disability, because I could end up taking care of him. It could affect his earning potential. "After all, you're in good health. Why take on such problems?"

Mom knew what she was talking about, too. Dad couldn't get a decent job after they married. One place found out he was Jewish and they fired him: Smucker's jam and jellies — a factory job. We never ate Smucker's in our house. Finally, he got a job in the post office. "Can you imagine that a man with a law degree can't get a job in this country?" Mom asked.

It wasn't David's deafness that got to me — it was our lovemaking. After our first encounter I told him, "I won't be seeing you anymore."

"Why?" He appeared shocked. He threw back his chin and head in disbelief. A night on his big mattress had probably cured many women of their ailments. In fact, I had picked up the phone that morning to hear a woman's voice plaintively asking for him. I quietly placed the phone on the receiver without ever telling him.

"You don't cuddle," I said softly.

"Oh, I didn't think you wanted to, but I know how to do that," he said.

The next time we made love, he snuggled me as if his life depended on it.

The following morning over breakfast, he said, "See, I can cuddle. Can we keep seeing one another?"

One Friday evening after a long week of my looking for a job, we were sitting on his mattress, ready for another grueling, luscious lovemaking session. Like all the other times, we had fallen into a pattern of eating his crackers and caviar, drinking his champagne in the early morning hours, then leaving separately at dawn.

"What do you think about getting married and having a child by next spring?" I asked him.

He looked dumbfounded.

"Is that what you want?" he asked incredulously.

"Yes. I am looking for Mr. Right. Surely, I can't keep on doing this forever with no commitment."

He laughed and looked me straight in the eyes. "I am not Mr. Right, but I'd be happy to hang out with you until Mr. Right comes along."

Why did I want to marry again after two bad tries?

I thought he was a pretty slippery character; but in a way, I was delighted with his cleverness. I just couldn't let this kind of intelligence go.

Mom was taking an interest in David. David was the only man that I had dated who actually knew how to talk to my mother. She was elated that he came from a Jewish family in New Jersey. He told her that he grew up on the same street as my Uncle Moe and my niece Miriam. He called her Sarah. All my other boyfriends seemed cowered by her, and called her Mrs. Perlman.

Dad even got into the act and told Uncle Moe that I was dating David.

"That Pitman kid — he ruined my lawn. He mowed off the tops of the grass, when he was fifteen," Uncle Moe generously volunteered.

These facts alone seemed to give David undue credibility, as if he had come over on the same boat from the old country. Finally, they could boast to our relatives that their daughter was dating a Jewish boy from the area, despite the fact that I had had three live-in boyfriends and incalculable casual encounters.

"We weren't spring chickens when we got married," Mom never failed to tell me when I got down about the single life.

I couldn't understand why they fell for David's soft-soaping.

The first thing David and I did when we moved in together was agree to have an open relationship. I didn't want to be controlled, nor did he. I strove to break every rule, and David heartily challenged me, and followed suit. We were used to having our cake and eating it too.

We went through many debilitating situations where we hurt each other — coming home smelling like someone else, or running into an overly zealous woman or man on the street while we were together. These would be followed by a firestorm of inquiries, tears, screaming and new expectations by both of us. He became more insulated, less communicative, while I became more invasive: going through his phone bill, wallet and pockets looking for clues.

If someone had asked me at that point what I wanted, I'd have said a monogamous relationship, but I sure didn't know how to create one, and after a while David and I were causing each other a lot of suffering.

I was learning a lot about men — one man in particular — in a way I had never learned before. I was also learning how to be in a relationship by testing every fear and defense I knew. It felt like an advanced course. David would say to me after we hauled off verbally and stood firm, "Do you want to be right or do you want to be in a relationship?"

"I want to be right!" I screamed back, but I knew that right beneath the words, I wanted to be in a relationship with him.

Mom asked me if we were ever going to get married. I didn't know. All I knew was that I couldn't let go of him. He was breaking me down in ways that I didn't fully understand. I just had to love him on faith.

Like the day I came home from work and found the house filled with women. "We're waiting to be interviewed by David," a strange attractive woman at my door told me. "You'll have to get at the end of the line."

"But I live here!" I insisted.

"Oh, come in then. We're all answering an ad from the *Independent Journal* for a Gal Friday for David."

I finally located him out on the deck, in deep concentration, listening to an interviewee talk about how she loved to work with people. He looked up and smiled when he saw me. "Oh, hi."

"What is going on here?" I asked indignantly, feeling invaded by young, attractive, well-dressed women with résumés.

"They're answering my ad," he said.

"Are you giving them a typing test?" I asked.

"Do you think I should?"

"Isn't that part of the job?"

"Well, yes, but I hadn't thought of it." He paused. "Could you help me out and do it for me?" He waved his hand to include all the waiting women.

I walked away disgustedly and went into our bedroom. There were two women sitting on our bed chatting pleasantly.

"Please!" I said exasperatedly.

"Oh, you can't cut in line. We're next," one said to me.

"I LIVE HERE!"

"Oh." They both got up and left to join the line out in the living room.

Once, I found him over at a girlfriend's house late at night. I knew they had slept together. Another time, I sneaked back to the house to see if he had kept his promise to stay home the night I went out. Finally, I slept with our landlord to get even with him for sleeping with my girlfriend.

We screamed and yelled hateful words at each other. Finally the old lady upstairs couldn't stand it any longer and called the police. We looked at each other: were we what they called a case of domestic violence? We thought we were just working it through. But it had gotten too intense, even for us.

We grew exhausted from the fighting. What were we so angry about? He didn't want to be hemmed in or controlled. He said he felt like he was dying in the relationship. I wanted a commitment and wouldn't take no for an answer. It was true that we both had been married before. It wasn't as if it was new territory. Finally, I gave him an ultimatum.

"Here it is: Number One Option: We get married. Number Two: We call it a California growth experience and move on before we murder each other."

And why was it so difficult for me? Women with less intelligence, less charm and less beauty had found husbands, and enjoyed the benefits of marriage. Surely I, too, could succeed in this basic endeavor. I longed to master this rite of passage, and move on with my life.

After six years of living together, when push came to shove, he didn't want to get married after all.

"*Nu?* (What's new?) *Boobbe-myseh!* (Nonsense!) Why buy the cow, when you can get the milk for free?" Mom reminded me again when I told her my bad news.

I decided to move out, and live where I wanted to live regardless of David. I didn't want to move from the waterfront where we were, so I chose an apartment a block away. I didn't realize until I moved in to the place that through the window over the kitchen sink, I could see directly into to our old bedroom.

I was determined never to talk to him again and I immediately set out on a program to forget him. A friend gave me the name of a Jewish matchmaker.

Her housekeeper ushered me in. She greeted me in her terry cloth bathrobe as she came directly from her lap pool. Francie Steinbrenner looked like an aging Shirley McLaine.

"Honey, women come three ways," she said as she greeted me. "They are like cars: big outdated Packards, cute old Studebakers and trendy sports cars. You, my darling, *shayna maidel* (pretty Jewish girl) are a sports car!"

I had passed the test. I was still a marketable item. I had a chance to finally get and stay married. She introduced me to several dozen eligible bachelors in Marin County. One even asked me to marry him on the first date. I was repulsed! But he was a lawyer. I called my mother. She said, "He must have a dark secret to pop the question that soon — reject him!"

"But Mom, you only knew Dad for three months!"

"That was then, this is now."

Finally after a month on the singles' circuit, I broke down and called David. "It's hard to lose a boyfriend and a best friend at the same time," I said into his message machine.

He called me right back. He had been napping on his mattress on the floor, since I had taken the bed frame and all my furniture.

Then David's father suddenly took ill and he rushed back to be with him. David spent much of that year traveling back and forth to the East Coast.

He told me that his dad, close to death, asked him about me. "What does she mean to you?"

"She's my best friend," David said.

"Then what are you waiting for?" his dad asked. Two days later he died in David's arms. David told me this with tears in his eyes but no marriage proposal.

I had never lived alone, but I learned to stay with myself in that beautiful apartment on the bay, hearing the fog horns moan in the early hours, partnering with Pussypie, my cat, as the winter rains pounded the roof. I felt the horror of being alone for the first time, and the joy of it. I set up my easel to paint. Something I had been doing on and off all my life. But I couldn't paint. I would awake in the middle of the night, fear riddling my bones. My watch-cat's ears would perk up as she stared at me — red alert — an intruder. Later, we both discovered it was the sound of the icemaker extruding ice cubes in the refrigerator.

One night, Pussypie found a slew of field mice that had come in from the cold nesting on top of the refrigerator. She woke me in the dead of night by chasing them around the living room.

My call to David had rekindled our courtship. Late one night, he carried his pillow and blanket one block and entered my house.

Pussypie greeted him like an old friend. I could see that they had really missed one another. The fighting stopped. Before, she would yelp and meow when we fought, like a frightened child. Now she cuddled between us in bed, loudly purring.

I could afford this lease for only a year, because the rent was sapping my resources. Once again, I told David that I was going to move away. He asked me to move back in with him. Here I did my heaviest negotiations. "If I move back in, I want you to pay the rent, and we must get married in six months."

By the time we had carried over the furniture to the old place, it felt like I had never left. This had gone on deeper and longer than my marriages because I realized that this man could draw a line in the sand and I'd step over it. Then, he'd deal with me. The other men didn't have the voltage I needed.

Mom commented on how we kept our own money separate, how he had women friends, how we were so affectionate in public. But most of all on the day of our marriage Mom and

Dad beamed with pride. They showed up for the wedding and spent the week.

"I love your friends. They are so open and creative," Mom said in a surprised tone.

We spent less than a thousand dollars on the wedding. My dress cost one hundred, on sale. I was so grateful to finally marry David that I let go of any dreams I had of impressing anyone with a big, brassy affair.

For days before, he suffered from migraines. He told me that he might not be able to go through with it. I was afraid he would stop the wedding right in the middle and back out. That Sunday in mid-August, the rabbi took him aside and spent an hour calming him down. I felt like I was having a mental meltdown, but I decided to keep it to myself. We had invited thirty-two people who all knew each other. David planned the whole thing and designed the ceremony. We had two rabbi friends marry us, and two pastors of the church on the hill overlooking the bay. Later we all went back to our apartment for a buffet. Sharon gave us the toast.

"We weren't sure if you guys were going to kill each other or marry each other!" she announced. Everyone laughed.

On our official wedding night, "official" because we had logged in a lot of sleeping together time in six years, I had a dream that my mom and Aunt Helen were downstairs in the living room discussing my having a child. They were even naming the child without me. Mom was calling it *Beshert* (a gift). I was upstairs in the attic painting a picture. Suddenly, I felt a little spirit inside me, and I also knew that this baby would be a gift for my mother. But suddenly, I deeply felt that I wasn't ready for this spirit wanting to impregnate me. I wanted to express myself through my art. And so the spirit left as quickly as it had come.

The next week I received a hand-written letter from my mom:

Dearest Daughter of my heart,
    We were looking forward to seeing you and being at your wedding for the last six years. The day finally arrived. A beautiful, magnificent day. You picked a glorious day to be married. Let it be a good omen!
    The service was beautiful and meaningful. You looked very happy and your friends appeared to be sharing your happiness.
    For us, the week flew by. What a wonderful week. Thanks to you!
    Our wishes for you are the very best of good health, happiness, success and a long life together.
    We look back on our marriage, and we have had our ups and downs, but our love for each other has never wavered. We have gotten angry with each other, and frustrated, but we have always simmered down, talked about our differences and made compromises. You must work at marriage always.
    Have a honeymoon! Enjoy! Enjoy!
    We love you, Mom and Dad

That day put Mom and me on equal footing. It didn't seem to matter that I was childless, or that David wasn't really her type. Or perhaps, my restlessness had beaten them down so much that they were just grateful I wasn't lying in some alley in the city, shooting up on drugs.

David and I no longer accepted the old ways of being with each other. We gradually cleared away the wreckage of the past and clarified a vision of what it was we wanted together. I overheard him say to a friend, "There's nothing in it for me to keep hurting her." We had become each other's teachers.

After years of proclaiming my independence and self-reliance, I had arrived at the same place as Mom. We both cherished our men, and acknowledged that their love propelled us into the world with confidence.

Marriage was the most mysterious covenant in the universe. There seemed to be no two alike; even a single marriage changed from day to day. Time felt like a significant factor — sometimes even more important than love. There were times when I thought that our coming together was a kind of accident, that we had wedded because of a string of incidents. Or was it really destiny? As we got to know one another, we had conversations about how we could have met half a dozen times before, just living our lives, one concentric circle away from the other, but didn't.

Sometimes I would lie awake and look at him asleep next to me, and think — Why, he's still here, after all these years. How strange, and what a miracle.

2

When Dad first stepped into the condo that David and I shared in Tiburon, his mouth dropped open. He took in how the structure hung over the waters of Raccoon Straits with a panoramic view of Angel Island and the Golden Gate Bridge — a far cry from the asphalt of Newark, New Jersey.

"Oh, so dis must be one of them-there condomoniums," Dad quipped, imitating Archie Bunker from "All In The Family."

I am remembering this when the plane banks, gaining altitude. The pilot's voice, deep and cottony, comes on the loud speaker. "Thank you for flying with us today. We'll be cruising at an altitude of thirty-seven thousand feet. To your left, you'll see the coastline of California. We're lucky to have clear visibility and calm skies. Notice how the coastline is a lighter shade of beige than the land. It juts out like a long fingernail over the Pacific Ocean." His voice, sounding like Chuck Yeager, instills confidence in me.

I press my nose against the window and look down through the puffy clouds. My dad, a consummate fatalist, would often say, "Buy land in Denver now, because when 'The Big One' comes, you'll have valuable ocean property."

But looking down at this thin ledge, where half the population of California makes its home, is like gazing into a blazing fire — at once compelling and terrorizing. I only had a vague notion of what was being assembled for me three thousand miles away on that warm July evening as I closed my eyes and relaxed back into my seat, remembering Dad's sense of humor.

My mother's panicky voice on my answering machine punctures the quiet early morning air. "Honey, come home immediately," Mom had said. "Dad was rushed to the hospital last night. I'll be waiting for you in the intensive care unit at St. Barnabas in Livingston." Her panic sets off mine, and immediately I am worried.

David shifts his large wiry frame on the bed as he frowns at me, his gray hair crushed close to his head from sleep.

At first, I am oddly ambivalent about making the trip back to New Jersey. Then, suddenly, I realize if Dad dies and I am not at his bedside, I will never forgive myself.

I *must* see him. I *must* let him know by this one act that I love him despite our long history of anger, his silences, his stinginess with emotions, and his lack of interest in my life that spans my fifty years and his eighty, because my lifestyle wasn't what he wanted for me.

I call back my childhood phone number I still know by heart, and leave a message that I will meet her at the hospital late that evening.

David drives me to the airport. The empty shops and stucco-housed windows along 19th Avenue reflect the emptiness and gloom I feel at the prospect of leaving him and facing this situation alone. He buried his mom and dad several years ago, and now it may be my turn. I feel him touch my hand in the shadows, and realize how much I take him for granted after twenty years of marriage. I gently rub the back of his neck, feeling anxious about leaving him. I didn't ever think that I could find a man like him to love, or that we would ever feel this bonded to each other.

The half-full plane takes off at exactly seven o'clock and passengers draw deep into themselves to sleep. The atmosphere is quiet and dark. I doze off, then awake with a start and begin turning this crisis over in my mind like a dog gnawing on a dry bone. I know Dad has Parkinson's and gall bladder problems. What do I know about loss or death? My close call with breast cancer three years earlier? My endless string of live-in boyfriends, two failed marriages, and nameless one night-flings in the 'sixties?

At Newark Airport, I grab the first taxi I see. The long drive seems excruciatingly slow. Finally we arrive at the gray concrete building that is St. Barnabas Hospital.

I run in the automatic front doors, and assault the ageless woman behind the desk. "I'm looking for Saul Perlman."

She considers the list before her, and then looks up at me over her bifocals. "He's in ICU, on the fourth floor."

"Oh God, please. . . ." I say a prayer as I hurry toward the elevator.

My mom spots me first; she is standing outside his room. She greets me with a wordless hug. I press into her five-foot-one sturdy frame, relieved that I made it through time and space. An invisible cord connects us. This unnamable hole inside me that aches with loneliness — a feeling that I've learned to live with and even ignore, in the name of growing up, being an adult — is suddenly gone. She has always been inside me. Her body is flaccid and yielding.

She leads me in. We stop for a moment as she carefully puts a blue paper mask over her thinning, strawberry-blonde-dyed hair and secures it around her mouth. I put one on too. We approach his bed.

22

I see my father's clouded eyes and hear his rasping breath. He looks up, small and gray. He smiles at me. "Hello, Honey, how are you?"

I feel I'm breathing for the first time in twelve hours. I can't take it all in. He's alive, old, gray and undone. My mind takes over: the executive function. I don't want to feel this. I have to stay in control. If I break down they will ridicule my weakness — something they detest in me. He's alive. This is a temporary condition. He'll walk out of here tomorrow. My dad is tenacious.

"I'm okay, Dad. How are you?"

"Hanging in there," he whispers. "How was your trip?"

I reach for his hand. It feels cool and dry.

"It was okay."

He keeps beaming at me. "I love you, Sweetheart," he says gently, and closes his eyes.

Out of the clear blue, every now and then, Dad has said this. As if he's pulled himself out of his own fog to suddenly see me. He said it the day I graduated college probably because he was relieved that I made it through.

The room has a faint fragrance of my mother's Shalimar, and a smell like burning towels rising from my father's skin. He lies inert, with clear plastic tubes burrowed into holes in his neck and forearms; more tubes disappear under the sheets that cover his shrunken form.

Just then, the doctors arrive. My father opens his hard, small, brown eyes again and attempts to joke with them as they crowd around his bedside.

"I'll treat you to lox and bagels when I get out of here," he rasps through his respirator. "Let me just run home and take a shower, and I'll come right back."

"Such a wise guy," my mother says to no one in particular. She rests in a metal chair she has pulled over to the side of the bed. He smiles at her and then he beams at me.

I feel relieved to hear him joking. See, he is just here for the weekend. Playing around, my old dad. Can't keep him down. My mom plays the straight man to his George Burns Jewish schtik. He'll be out in no time.

A doctor takes me aside, away from my mother's hearing. I am surprised at his singling me out. After all, I am just the daughter.

"I am Dr. Arnstein." He says. His smile is purely professional. From his six-foot broad-shouldered frame, he looks down at me and I feel like a small girl.

"And your husband, did he come with you?" he inquires.

"No," I responded. "He's back in California."

I felt myself getting defensive. He is broad-shouldered and has gray hair and glasses, but he appears to be around my age.

"He had to work today," I continue, then am irritated at myself. I am lying. Maybe I read too much into his remark. Did he have some expectation about my husband being here, something Mom said to him that I don't know about?

Mom and David keep a respectful distance from one another, and their feelings are hidden. David circumvents her controlling grip by remaining unavailable and elusive. She's happy that he's Jewish and after two of my bad tries, delighted that I've finally settled down. She's afraid to ask anything more of him. Maybe she'll scare him away.

Dr. Arnstein senses my annoyance, and looks at me carefully. His arms are crossed in front of him.

"Let me explain something to you. Your mother needs all the support and help she can get right now. I've seen women like her before, all energy and support and then less than a year after their husbands go, they suddenly give out, too. Your dad is in very unstable condition. He is having trouble breathing. His lungs have failed him. So we put him on a respirator. The machine is doing it for him, and the trac in his throat helps him push the air out for him to form words and talk."

"What happened?" I asked.

"He had a gall bladder attack and his intestines perforated. We are treating him for septicemia. He can expire at anytime, or hang on for several months — enough time to wear down an eighty-year-old woman like your mother. It's a miracle your father's still with us. We had to revive him twice. The advanced Parkinson's and his age weakens any real chance for full recovery."

I learned the hard way not to go against my mother's wishes or she would make my life miserable. I couldn't possibly fight with her about pulling the plug. Besides, this doctor didn't know about my dad's stubborn will. If my mom wanted him to live — he would live, and that's all there was to it.

"Does he have a living will?" he asked.

"No," I answered. In my family we don't discuss these things. What he truly doesn't understand is that my mother has never been sick a day in her life, and she wouldn't give out now, because she has a cause. It has always been expected that my dad would go first. He didn't know how to boil water or take care of himself. Mom waited on him hand and foot. Mom was an adult at the age of eleven, working as a cashier for her dad's delicatessen on the Lower East Side. It is unthinkable that my mother would die, much less Dad.

"At this point, the machines are keeping him alive. Not everyone wants to live under these conditions."

I feel very heavy. My cotton blouse and the waistband of my pants are pressing tightly against my stomach. I feel bloated, old and irritated. Dad is alive! He isn't dead. You don't know *my* dad. He'll get better. I stare into this stranger's eyes.

He shifts his body, as if to get a better foothold on the situation, and continues, "I don't want to revive him again, if he has heart failure. Your mother insists that we do. I want you to talk some sense into her. She must let him go, so he can die with dignity. Otherwise if we do another code blue on him, the machine will be breathing a clinically dead man."

I feel angry with Dr. Arnstein. He is arrogant and cocky. He doesn't know what he is talking about. He doesn't know that my family survives on sheer will and anxiety. *Kenahora* (melodrama) is our middle name.

I return to my dad.

The doctors surrounding my dad appear to like his pleasantness. It makes it easier for them. They have seen this drama many times before. I see it in their eyes.

Mom gestures for me to join her out in the hall, then gives me the key to Dad's Buick. "Get a copy made, so you can drive the car," she whispers to me. "But don't tell Dad."

I accept this obediently. Besides, it gives me more elbow room in this developing crisis. Deception, a little deception was always tolerated against unsuspecting Dad. Our core secret acknowledged — men were a little dense, anyway.

They have been married fifty-seven years, and we all understand that the car is his domain.

When I was sixteen and showing off my driving permit, I asked Dad, "Why won't you let Mom drive?"

"I'm in charge of domestic politics, financial affairs and the car. Your mom is in charge of the feeling department and the kitchen," he answered matter-of-factly.

Of course, growing up, it sure looked that way to me, but later I came to resent his lack of flexibility, his intolerance and the double standard between my brother and myself.

Back at the house, I open the trunk of my dad's car. Dampness and mildew fill my nostrils. Inside, I find a long-handled snow shovel, rusty tire chains and a large, worn, brown shopping bag filled with road maps of New Jersey. I look at them closely. Some go back to before the Garden State Parkway was built in the late nineteen-fifties. I cart these to the trashcan.

I wonder if he will ever drive again. I glance around the neglected yard and feel that something is shifting inside of me. I make a note to get someone to clean the fallen twigs and leaves in the yard before I go back to California. When I was little, I helped my dad rake and burn these leaves in the gutters outside the front of the house in late fall and early winter. Suddenly, I miss that woody smoky smell that defined autumn on the East Coast.

I feel like I'm breaking and entering. The winter air makes the houses and trees look like crystal against the cobalt sky.

I return to the car, sit behind the wheel fooling with the automatic buttons on the steering wheel. My car doesn't have all these electronic gizmos. I'm fascinated.

This was where Dad and I used to have our worst fights and where we shared our best secrets. When he taught me how to drive, he practically jumped out of his seat and had a stroke each time I got to an intersection. He kept stomping on the floorboards, afraid I wasn't stopping in time.

Once, when he picked me up from school, I heard a love song playing on the car radio and asked him, "Why do so many people sing about love?" He turned towards me, paused and slowly answered, "Dear, some people think that love is the most important emotion in the world."

He probably thought so, but like most men of his generation, he'd never admit it. I was too young to think to ask him this obvious question. Adolescent puppy love, "Moon River," "Suddenly Last Summer" — for me love was the only worthwhile emotion, but still just out of my grasp. Not like today, where romantic love is grounded in the realities of the cliché but it's a workaday world. Life has used me, romantic love is easy work compared to the hard realities of waking up with the same man for twenty years. Only now do I have a glimmer of understanding of what love really is. Watching my mother and father that day after fifty-seven years of marriage made me a believer in the devotional aspects of the institution. "I am devoted to your mother," he would say when I asked him if he loved her, never, "I love your mother."

Through the rear view mirror of the car, I look at three elementary school kids walking home. I feel like I am seven years old, scared and not ready for this crisis.

I drive back to the hospital and join a line of cars waiting to pick up passengers. The heavy automatic doors of the main entrance to St. Barnabas slide open and closed, open and closed, as each wave of visitors and patients enter and exit. Some, I think, are transported to the morgue downstairs and taken out by men in gray suits from the nearby mortuaries, whose business signs and billboards dot the streets of Essex County: Smith and Jones; McFarlane, O'Flanagan and Lynch; Cohen and Bernstein.

My mother is waiting inside the entrance on this raw overcast afternoon in January, as I put the car in park and sit at the curb of the main entrance to the hospital.

Through the glass doors, I see the small frame of a woman in a beige raincoat with a fur collar. She appears gray and old. No one else would notice her, but I focus on her and try to memorize the scene. She is my mother. I feel my heart lurch with pain.

Next to her, three new mothers in wheelchairs wait for their husbands to drive around and pick them up. Newborn babies are buried deep and secure in blankets in their laps. Bobbing in the air above them, caught by the draft of the door, pink and blue helium balloons are tied to the arms of the wheelchairs. Absent-eyed and dazed, the mothers watch the sliding glass door opening and closing.

Only my mother and I are playing out some sad drama in which I am the actress, the audience and the author. It feels like we have been preparing for this moment for years.

I wave. Mom sees me. Since I arrived early this morning, tears have been forming deep inside me. I want to connect with her. I want her attention, her warmth. I am frightened of the dark, the emptiness and what is unfolding in our lives.

She comes out the door and slowly gets in. The sun sinks behind the South Mountain Reservation, leaving us in dusky winter light. At that moment, I remember how I hate this town, this time of year, and this time of day. I want to be somewhere else, in a different place in my life.

"This weather is crummy," she agrees. She has a habit of reading my mind. Once, when I confronted her on this, she replied soberly, "It's my job, I am your mother."

How I resented her. She was my jailer. Now I can laugh at her bluntness. I needed her control. I was an impulsive, willful child. She saw me in a way I could not see myself. She'd yell, "You have to learn the hard way, always the hard way. You're *fartumelt* (confused)."

"How about taking a spin around Saks?" I suggest.

She giggles, but says, "We probably should get home in case the night nurse calls about Dad." However, I can see she's tempted.

"We won't be long, just a spin, maybe they'll be showing some early spring stuff," I continue. My request comes out of denial of what's unfolding, but also because I want to create something familiar and intimate between us. I know it would do us both good to have a little normalcy return to our lives.

I feel her hesitate. Finally she succumbs.

"Okay, dear."

"I knew it wouldn't take much!" We laugh together now conspiratorially as I point the car down Old Short Hills Road.

I feel her mood shift. I turn toward her briefly and see her smile and settle happily back into her seat. "I'm so glad to see you, Dear. I am so worried about Dad. I just want him to get better." She is thinking out loud.

We pass Dr. Arnstein's house. I recognize it from the doctor shingle hanging outside near the curb. Next to it is his wife's name, Dr. Naomi Arnstein.

My mother looks at me. I feel her eyes.

"What?" I say a bit too sharply.

"I thought you would have all this by now." She nods her head at the matching signs, and the imposing red brick house set far back from the street. It has white trimmed window sashes and shutters and a massive front door.

We drive on in silence deepened by the darkening sky. I think about her unspoken expectations for me to marry a doctor, raise a family and live close to her. Even now, though I'm successful as a financial planner, I still feel like I am a disappointment to her.

I park Dad's Buick Riviera in the back of Saks in the handicapped zone, and place my dad's placard on the dashboard.

Slowly my mother lifts one leg and then the other out of the car. She wears little cushiony Nike sneakers. They looked like white glazed donuts attached to the bottom of her ankles — out of place with her woolen sport jacket and A-line skirt.

"We've got to stop at the shoe department first," she proclaims. New life seems to come back into her body as she marches ahead of me to the entrance. "Mr. Alpert put aside some samples for me before Dad took ill."

She pulls open the large glass doors and strides to the shoe department at the far side of the building. I find myself rushing to keep up with her short, quick pace. In a moment, she has

30

seated herself in one of the chairs, her foot extended, trying to get Mr. Alpert's attention.

He flashes a smile at her to let her know he'll be right with her. "Oh, Sweetheart, he's got some Amalfi's that are just my size."

Her excitement is contagious. I begin to sense the bliss of shopping, the needing, the wanting, the finding, the selecting, the total attentiveness of the salesperson. "Good choice," he might say, or "Just lovely," as he hands you your package in a shopping bag, the receipt tucked safely inside. I love the attention, quick to strike up a conversation and instant friendship with strangers, where Mom and I are in charge. So unlike the hospital, where I feel like a profes-sional victim — people scatter when I ask for something.

Mr. Alpert has waited on my Mom for years. He saves all the sample shoes just for her size five foot. He is the only other man my mother has a thing for — the thing is shoes.

"Well, Mrs. Perlman, how are you today?" Mr. Alpert coos. "Is this your lovely daughter?"

"Yes," my mother says proudly. "She's visiting from San Francisco." She pronounces San Francisco the way one pronounces the name of a foreign city.

"Oh, Frisco! I have a friend out that way," he replies as he goes to get the shoes he has been saving for my mother.

I know exactly what they will look like before Mr. Alpert brings them out. My mother has dozens of tiny pairs like these at home, lining the closet floor: Amalfi's, Bruno Magli, Enzo Angiolino, Franco Sarto and Ferragamo. They are all sling-back, open toe, no higher than a one-inch heel.

My mother started her collections of Gucci purses, Natori nightgowns and designer shoes when she was finally able to sell the deserted forty acres her mother owned for years. "Our ship will come in," she would say wistfully. After years of heartache trying to sell it, they got a whopping half-million from a developer. When I asked her what she wanted to do with the money, she said angrily, "Pay all the taxes on it."

"No, for yourself?" I pushed for an answer.

"Buy myself a Gucci bag."

"But Mom, that's only one or two hundred dollars at the most," I said.

Over the years, her one Gucci bag grew into several dozen, and the Amalfi shoes grew as well. A small price for the deprivation she endured as a child. As these collections grew, I saw the little girl in her come alive.

The world feels familiar, secure, and normal again. The past forty-eight hours melt away. Mom and I are happily doing what we always do together: shop.

"You're coming to Maui with us, when Dad gets better?" I ask cautiously.

"Oh honey, we're looking forward to it! He will be out of the hospital by then, at the very least," she responds. She nods and waves Mr. Alpert away to wrap up the shoes without trying them on.

With a wide smile, Mr. Alpert hands her the three pairs of shoes in a large black shopping bag with Saks scrawled in red on both sides. We make our way into the women's department.

I draw her attention to a soft, ankle-length, white silk skirt with a beige banana leaf pattern on it. I can see she is interested. We look for her size and find it right away. I hold it up for her to see. She touches the hem and seams and examines how it is made.

"This will be just perfect for our Maui trip, Dear." She hands the salesgirl her MasterCard.

We chat, we touch, we stroll down the aisles, we spot things that the other might like, feeling them and holding them up to admire. On the way out I admire a mannequin wearing a long, slinky, midnight-blue silk Versace gown with a feathered hem.

"Oh, buy it! *That* would look great on you," Mom says cheerfully as she fingers the silk material. I bend to touch the feather hem. We examine the price tag.

"Only twenty-five hundred dollars, Mom," I laugh. "You love to spend my money!" We leave Saks without the dress.

We drive back home down the dark roads of Millburn. The streetlights sparkle as the frosty night air creates a shimmery glow around each one.

Our house is painted in blackness as we pull into the driveway. The excitement of Saks evaporates. It is not like old times, after all.

In the light of the open car door, I catch an image in the rear view mirror. A fifty-year-old woman I don't recognize stares back at me. What is she doing driving my father's car?

3

The automatic sensor light goes on over the garage, illuminating the driveway and throwing the back of the house into patterns of stark black night and white icy shadows. I get out of the car, leaving my mom in the passenger seat, and unlock the wooden garage doors. The garage is piled high with boxes of Dad's newspaper clippings and mildewed bundles of old *New York Times* Sunday magazines. Over the years, these cartons have spread like kudzu. They've completely overtaken the space, so that the car slips in tightly, almost grazing the boxes. Mom and I have just enough room on either side to squeeze out. The familiarity of the ritual of putting the car in and the emptiness in my stomach without Dad grip me.

Over the years, these bundles have set Mom and me to joking about Dad's obsession for cutting clippings and filing stories that he wanted to re-read after he retired. It took him the first six months of his retirement to go through all the boxes, and then he had nothing to do. But tonight, we don't mention it.

Mom waits for me while I get the packages, and then we automatically walk down the short concrete path that leads to the back of the house. The front door is for guests.

We pass the pachysandra that Mom planted the year we moved in. Although it is winter, it still creeps the wrong way despite all her attempts to train it to grow away from the sun to cover an unsightly concrete slab.

The gray painted wood stairs creak as we step carefully to avoid icy patches. Mom turns her key in the lock and we enter the house. I'm overcome with sadness that Dad is not here. Perhaps she feels it, too. But her face is expressionless.

Mom scurries around, turning on the lamps in the den and the living room, raising the thermostat in the dining room, dropping her Saks bag on the landing to take upstairs later.

Ripening bananas in a bowl on the kitchen table and the pungent odor of garbage in the bin under the sink fill my nostrils. The stagnant air begins to stir.

"Can I make you something to eat?" she asks when she comes back in the kitchen.

It seems much too late to eat, yet the familiarity of the cluttered kitchen tempts me. I nod.

She grabs her apron and ties a knot around her thick waist in one quick move.

Out come the Heinz's ketchup, mustard and seltzer water. She puts them on the small wood kitchen table and sets a place for me with great speed and efficiency.

In seconds, a cold platter of leftover roasted potatoes, a pan filled with beef brisket and a tin plate with half an apple pie appears. "You won't mind leftovers?" she asks rhetorically. "It'll just take a minute to warm them up."

"I'll take my luggage upstairs."

I pick up my bag and enter the cluttered sanctuary of the living room. A huge portrait of my dad hangs over the fireplace. It dwarfs the three French provincial couches, two wingback, upholstered armchairs, and two mahogany tables in a space no larger than a doctor's waiting room.

At the top of the stairs, I stop. Ahead of me are three open green bedroom doors: my brother's room, my parents' room, and mine. It amazes me that the four of us lived in such a tiny house for nineteen years. Another part of me watches with a hollowness inside. A familiar dampening-down feeling is seeping into every pore. I believe the story I tell myself now: nothing is wrong. We are a happy family. But I can't extinguish the deep dread I feel of being back in this house and peering into these rooms again.

In the darkness of my bedroom, I grope for the light switch. Suddenly, I'm in a time warp. The room is exactly as it was when I was an adolescent; I call it "My Memorial Library and Archives." The wallpaper is little rose buds on a green-and-white background framed in enamel high gloss baseboards, doors and door frames. The vanity, surrounded with a white gathered taffeta skirt, displays photos in silver frames of me in my first high school formal, a strapless orange chiffon dress, with Larry Sockman. In another photo, my brother and I are smiling with the Bradley Beach seashore as a backdrop. A mirrored tray behind the photos displays half-full perfume bottles and lotions. I see the sediment inside the bottle of Channel No. 5. I open it and the smell stuns me. I am back at the eighth grade dance in the temple gym, jitterbugging to Bill Haley and the Comets, my gray-and-pink felt poodle skirt twirling. I am held in turns by Larry Leberman, the brain, Sandy McHallagher, the football player, and Barry Herner, my grade-school flame.

The fragrance brings me back to Johnny Mathis's dreamy voice lulling me to sleep in my single bed, while the white chiffon curtains rustle in the humid summer night breeze. I will live forever. I know that most surely, as I also know that my future is filled with so much promise.

The record player is still on the floor near the closet. My books from high school are next to the bed: *Johnny Tremain,*

My Antonia, Anne of Green Gables, Shakespeare and the poems of Edna St. Vincent Millay.

Some of my knick-knacks have been carefully set to one side on the desk: a wooden monk praying, a plastic valentine doll with a red taffeta skirt and a hand-stenciled pillow. Right at the edge of my memory, I can place which boyfriend gave me each of these things. The valentine doll has a loose head from the time my brother smashed all the things in my room.

It started out like any other fight. He was teasing me about a guy in his class, and then he asked me about a girl he admired. I retorted, "Why would she care about you?" He lifted the hammer he had been using on a carpentry project and aimed for my head. I ducked, and it landed on my valentine doll. I started screaming like you wouldn't believe, while he came after me. Mom ran up the stairs yelling, "Saul, Saul, he's going to kill her!" She was hysterical for days and couldn't stop talking about how we had an axe murderer in the family. Dad threatened Harry with all kinds of punishment if he ever tried that again. Me, I was just plain scared of Harry after that.

"Dear, the food is ready! Come on down," Mom calls.

I leave the light on, quickly change into sweat clothes and wash up. As I descend the stairs, sweet odors of baked brisket and potatoes with onions greet me.

We sit and eat in silence. I sop up the gravy from the brisket with rye bread. I rarely eat meat in California, but my belly needs to feel full tonight.

"Doctor Arnstein wants me to take him off the respirator. I don't know what to do. Harry says that I should let him die with dignity," Mom says with an unspoken demand. I do not answer, and there is a wedge of silence between us.

"I can't let Dad go," she continues. "What would you do, Honey? Could you pull the plug on David?"

Mom had a way of letting you know the only right answer to a question.

Confined, tied to tubes and at the mercy of nurses and doctors, I couldn't allow myself to imagine what it was like for my dad. How could he possibly endure it?

It would be so clear what to do for an eighty-year-old man if I were back home in California. There I could be cold and efficient, the master of my life. Once, David told me that I became cold and distant when I knew his mother was dying. A firewall protecting my heart cuts me off from Dad's agony, but I soften for a split second toward Mom. I want to feel that softness all the time, like David, but I get frightened and overwhelmed, and close down.

"I don't know how I'd feel or what I would do if it were David," I say quietly. This seems to satisfy her. I see her eyes moisten. But then the phone rings, shattering the moment. Mom picks up the receiver.

"Oh, hello. How are you? Are you all right? When will you be here? We are waiting for you." Her voice is cool. "Meet us at the hospital tomorrow. We'll be on the fourth floor. Do you want to talk to your sister?" She hands the phone to me.

I take the phone and hold it in the air, at first, then slowly put it to my ear. I'm irritated that Mom assumes I can't wait to talk to my brother. I wonder what will come out of my mouth.

"Hi, Harry. Yeah, I got in about six today. It's been a long day. When will we see you?" I try to speak casually.

"Oh, uh, tomorrow, I guess," he says.

There is a long pause. My brother and his long, confounding pauses.

"I'll see you then," I reply. The sound of his voice after so many years disturbs me. I feel confused. I want a big brother to lean on. I want a good big brother to protect and help me. My girlfriend Sharon has boasted about her three big brothers ever since I've known her. That's the way families should be. All the old distrust creeps back when I hear Harry's voice.

I hand the phone back to Mom.

She explains everything to him in great detail, as if it will help make meaning and offer some control over things that are out of control.

"Harry, I don't want to stay on the phone," she says, finally. "I'd better get off and call the hospital. Yes, he was stable when we left. Drive carefully. See you tomorrow. Give my love to Roberta and Francine."

Her meal goes uneaten as she dials the intensive care unit of St. Barnabas. The phone number has already found a place on a piece of paper tacked to the wall beside the phone.

"This is Mrs. Perlman. Is this Shirley? How is he doing?" I wait for some indication from Mom's face that he is okay. I feel like I am floating somewhere outside my body, overtired, raw, overwhelmed. I feel bloated inside my clothes, like a boiled chicken.

She hangs up and turns to me. Her face is drawn and tired.

"Shirley says he's having a restless night. He keeps asking for me. They gave him some medication to calm him down and help him sleep through the night."

Appearing deep in thought, she carries her dishes to the sink. I stand up and bring mine over. She scrapes and washes and I start to dry, an old ritual we fall into naturally.

"I don't know if Roberta will be coming up with Harry."

She means my brother's wife. We look at each other.

"Did he say?"

"No."

Just like my brother to keep things vague. I don't really want to have to deal with Roberta and my brother at the same time. My irritation is increasing. He acts so different when she is around, like nothing bothers him. Like everything is fine, even when it's not. Roberta can be dancing nude on the breakfast nook table, and Harry will act like everyone's wife is expected to do that.

Zaftig was the word my dad used to describe her because of her wild, black-dyed shoulder-length hair and her robust torso with pendulous breasts. My dad, who silently tolerated everyone, didn't like her, but he never let her know.

"Did I tell you that she put me on hold the last time I called long distance, and then she forgot about me. Can you believe it?" Mom wipes her forehead with a soapy hand.

"The daughter-in-law gene," I mutter, sure that my irritation is showing from the way Mom hands me the phone, assuming I want to talk to Harry. Not that I shouldn't talk to him, but I just wasn't prepared to deal with him at that moment. And now I might be seeing both of them really soon.

"What?"

"Oh you know, every mother seems to be irritated by her daughter-in-law," I say lightly, trying to make a joke out of it. "Women are probably sitting on porches all over America complaining about their daughter-in-laws."

She didn't laugh. "I don't know what is wrong with you!" she said. "I try to tell you something serious, and you make fun. Why is everything so funny to you? You're *farblondjet* (mixed up)!"

Sometimes talking to my mother is like walking through a field of land mines. I never know when I step on something explosive. I try to recoup. "I know how you feel, Mom, but she tries very hard to get it right," I answer. "Maybe your standards are too high?"

I don't really know how hard Roberta is trying, but I am being contrary with Mom because she made me talk to Harry when I didn't want to. I better stop it now, I reason, or I am really going to have a fight on my hands. I am just as confused by Roberta as my mother. Sometimes I am downright offended by her behavior. First she talks down to me, then she won't give me the time of day.

Mom ignores my question and continues talking.

"The thing that really galls me is that she never calls me 'Mom'," she continues, her voice getting very intimate. "And then she even got angry at me for asking her why she wouldn't. She said, 'You aren't my mother'. But with such anger, *tchepping* me. It almost bowled me over."

"The woman is out of touch," I commiserate. I see on Mom's face that that is what is needed, so I continue. "Remember the time when Roberta and I went for a walk several Thanksgivings ago? It was the only time I've been alone with her, in all the years Harry has been married to her. We were walking down Plymouth Avenue and she told me that the reason she didn't like me was she thought I was the one who wanted Harry to get a divorce when she was hospitalized."

"You had nothing to do with it. You were three thousand miles away. Dad has always thought she was very unstable," Mom says.

Unstable is a good word for her, I think. My dad has a way of putting someone into a one-word picture frame.

Shortly after my brother and Roberta announced their engagement, she checked into a mental hospital treatment program. My parents were worried about the upcoming marriage. My dad asked me, "Doesn't a woman do something like that *after* she is married, not before?"

Dad's comment made it into a big family joke, on the Perlman side, that is. We didn't take her illness seriously because after all, my mother fixed Harry up with Roberta, so how crazy could she be? No one talked about a diagnosis. We all knew

Harry's eligible-bachelor status had always been an excuse for his introversion. As he moved into his forties, it was becoming difficult for him to hide behind that fact. I guess I thought they were like two bookends, complementing each other in a crazy way.

Then, when Francine was five, Roberta disappeared. When she returned disheveled and disoriented several days later, Harry was furious. Then she disappeared altogether. At first Harry thought she was having an affair, but some neighbors said they had seen her looking through garbage pails outside an upscale restaurant in Philadelphia. He went to look for her, but he could not find her.

She was gone for a year. Harry couldn't look after Francine and work at the same time, so he brought her up to New Jersey. Mom and Dad took care of her. They enrolled her in kindergarten at my old elementary school, and she had Miss August, my kindergarten teacher, who was ancient by then.

It was a bittersweet year for them, having a child to take care of. Mom walked little Francine to school each day, the only grandmother in a gaggle of young mothers. She was invited to class to teach the kids how to cook *latkes*.

One day a little boy teased Francine, "You don't have a mom." Overhearing this, my mom said, "Francine has a mother *and* a grandmother, and I'll punch out your lights if you tease her anymore!" Taking care of Francine seemed to give Mom and Dad new life, reliving the fun parts of parenting.

One Saturday, they took Francine to Alexander Graham Bell Laboratories Museum, where there were lots of old telephones on exhibit that kids could touch and play with.

"I thought she had forgotten about her mom, because she never said a word about her," Dad later related. But then he heard Francine make believe she was talking to her hospitalized mother on an old telephone. "Mom, come home. I love you and I miss you so much," she had said softly. As Dad related this story to me, tears ran down his face. Mom handed him her hankie. I was really moved by the story, because it told me something I always suspected. Deep in there was a very sensitive man, who had been hardened by his generation's idea of how men were supposed to behave.

Finally, Harry prevailed upon the rabbi at their temple to help. The rabbi tracked Roberta down and persuaded her to come home. But she was still disoriented and raving. Harry had her committed. They gave her electric shock treatment. It didn't help. Harry was beside himself. She was as wild and agitated as ever.

She did return, she totaled the car, walked away from the wreck, found her way home, and from that point on appeared normal. Occasionally, however, she still said or did strange things. The doctors speculated that "the brush with death" cured her, but no one knew for sure why "the cure" seemed to work.

"Roberta probably had no options," Mom told my father at the time. "Only a cruel man can make his wife fall off the edge like that. I told Harry, he has to be more understanding with her. He has to tell her he loves her more. He has to be more supportive." Mom told me that Harry said nothing but averted his eyes and hung his head.

Things changed imperceptibly after that with Mom and me. Maybe she decided that Harry hadn't done enough during this crisis, or maybe she saw what Roberta was capable of doing. Instead of saying that I contained raw, intense, untapped rage, ready to explode at her, there was a softening between us. I no longer felt the strange enmity that punctuated our relationship. It was true, I tried to be more sympathetic listening to her problems, but it surprised me more than anyone that I had this new second chance.

In my infrequent phone conversations with Harry, he let me know how much rage he felt toward Roberta for what she had done. She had publicly humiliated him with her bizarre behavior, something that he would never forgive.

Relatives have forgotten the details over time. Some may have thought of her behavior as just quirky. Like how she put little Hershey Kisses into birthday cards she sent. The cards were always late and the chocolate, crushed in transit, made the greetings unreadable. Then there was the way she never called anyone by name, or how she stuffed her closets with flea-market clothes. She had an insatiable appetite for clothes and jewelry, like I did when I was an adolescent.

"I wonder if they are giving your dad the right amount of medication?" Mom says absentmindedly, then pauses and hands me another dish. She changes the subject. "Harry is so mean to me."

My mother has a set of words unique to her. My girlfriends' mothers don't talk like this. *Mean* is one of those words. Baby words, words from 1929, like crummy, zoot suit, bilk, slip you a Mickey, or stingy.

"He doesn't give me any support. All he gives me are facts and meanness. I get no comfort from him!" she says. "Like the last time he came up. He drove me to the hospital, but he wouldn't park in the blue area with Dad's handicap sticker. He made me walk all the way across the icy parking lot to the front door. I can't believe that I raised a son to be this way!"

I quietly wipe the dishes, thinking it is good, it is him she is angry at, not me. Silently, I am spiteful and angry with my brother, and I have a pain in my heart for my mother.

I try to act neutral. I say, "I know, Mom," and continue wiping. I am walking on thin ice. If I side with her, she will soften; if I don't, she will attack me.

When she sees that this is all she will get from me, she changes the subject. "It is amazing how these young nurses do things these days. Everything is disposable and high-tech, not like it was when I was in nursing school."

At the age of eleven, a wave of pride washed over me one day in the attic when Mom showed me her nursing cape, cropped hat and nurse's pin. In the bottom of a metal armoire were photos of her as a protestor along with Margaret Sanger, old brochures for Planned Parenthood and materials supporting women's rights to use contraceptives. In 1952, while other mothers stayed at home cutting off the crusts of Wonder Bread to make school lunch sandwiches, my mom was an activist for Planned Parenthood. These were times when I was ashamed of her for not being like other mothers.

She interrupts my thoughts.

"Mrs. Nottingham has been working down at the five-and-ten again. She has been telling me that the woman that owns the store treats her like a dog. I told her to quit. 'You don't need this abuse, Dixy,' I tell her, but she doesn't listen."

I look over the sink windowsill out the window into Dixy Nottingham's living room. A woman, my mother's age, sits alone in an overstuffed armchair reading a book by the light of one table lamp. The rest of the house is in darkness.

"She's lucky that she has Dana and Dickie nearby since her husband died," Mom says. "We check in by phone when we don't see the light on in each other's house by night."

The strain of the day is beginning to sink in, and I want to sleep. I say good night and go up to my room and get into my bed, which seems smaller than I remembered it. But in spite of my fatigue, I am wide awake and restless. I'm afraid I won't be able to sleep after all. I throw off the blankets and walk into my Mom's room. She is undressing.

"Mom, can I sleep with you tonight?" My voice is tentative.

She smiles. "Yes, you can sleep on Dad's side."

I climb into their bed. Dad's body would know how to comfort her with his warmth. I wonder, after fifty-six years of marriage, the last time she and Dad slept separately. What is it like to go to sleep anxiously wondering if your husband will be gone when you awake?

"I need to watch television for awhile. It will calm me down," she says as she puts on her pale pink-challis nightgown.

I glance at her body, but trying not to stare. What does the eighty-year-old body of a woman look like? What do I have in store? She is built so differently than I am. She is big-chested but small-busted, with a strong torso, hips and belly, thin legs and tiny feet and hands, like a garlic bulb or a turnip growing close to the ground. Mom's side of the family is from Russian peasant stock. I must take after my dad, the Polish side.

She turns to me. "I am so worried about Dad."

"I know." I press my stomach and breasts against her back as soft as a pillow, and I wrap my arm around her thick waist, spoon-style. We have not done this since I was seven and crawled into bed on Saturday mornings with both of them. But I guess we both miss Dad so much, it feels right.

"You're such a cuddler, just like your Dad," Mom chuckles and allows me to snuggle closer. The television lulls us to sleep.

4

I awake disoriented. The sheets I'm lying on have a sweet, lingering smell of Mom. I remember that I am in Maplewood, and my dad is dying in the hospital. At that moment, I see my mom standing over me.

"Honey, please get up. I wanted you to sleep until the last minute, but we have to go now. The visiting hours at ICU are short, and we'll be late."

I jump out of bed, shower, and I'm downstairs in less than ten minutes. I'm irritated that she didn't wake me earlier, but I say nothing. I stand in front of her in the kitchen with wet hair and no makeup, but fully dressed and ready to go. I feel like I've been transformed back into her seventeen-year-old daughter.

My brother stands at the entrance to the ICU reception room. He is big and round. I look down, because my feelings confuse me. When I look at him, I see a sixteen-year-old face on a fifty-four year old man. I fold my arms in front of my chest. I am wary and uncomfortable.

He moves toward us. "Hi, Mom. Hi, Sis."

My mom hugs his large frame. He awkwardly pulls back.

"How was the traffic? Did you eat anything?" Mom asks, not expecting an answer.

I move to hug my brother. He feels stiff to my touch. It is brief and unsatisfying. He pushes away. His black shoes shuffle backward, and only seconds later does his flaccid frame follow.

"Let me find the doctor. Go inside and sit down. I'll come back and get you." Mom disappears down the airless white corridor.

After an interlude of many years, Harry and I are alone.

"When we die, he'll be the only family you'll have," Mom has said repeatedly over the years. It never mattered to me until now. Her statement is slowly sinking in. She doesn't understand why we aren't better friends; she was very close to her own brother.

As always, I make the first attempt. "So, Harry, what's been happening?" I try to sound cheerful.

"Oh, uh, nothing much. Work is going okay. My new boss is a black guy, okay? So he wants me to do this project, okay? But he gives it to three other guys. Oh, uh, so then I find out from talking to another guy that he is doing the same project. Okay?"

His self-conscious chatter irritates me. Can't he see that I am not interested? I keep noticing how he licks his lips when he speaks, and the strange way his tongue gets caught in his mouth when he forms certain words. Some come out filled with spit. Like the spit he used to wipe my face when I was five and he caught me putting my mother's powder on my cheeks in the bathroom. The spit he used as a weapon when we fought, when he cornered me in the vacant lot and tore at me, or humiliated me in front of his boyfriends. I try to wipe away this image by interrupting him.

"I got here yesterday," I tell him.

"So, what have you and Mom been doing?"

"We saw Dad yesterday, and then we went shopping. She bought a skirt that she is taking on our Maui trip."

"Your Maui trip? Oh! So you are all going on a vacation together?" he asks. "I can't understand it. You used to be the one they worried about. You couldn't even get a job with a college degree. *You* couldn't get your life together, but now *you're* the good one in the family. If I lived three thousand miles away, maybe *I'd* be the good one, too!" he says menacingly.

He's on the attack and I want to run away.

I try to protect myself from his criticism. I try to think of the images, my hard-won professional achievements — a book, a career, even a marriage, but he knows how to get to me. I imagine I wear a zipper that runs from my belly up to my neck; he could unzip me and take everything inside.

"So, Harry, what about Dad?" I ask, trying to hide my emotions.

Harry changes his stance. He stands up straighter now. I remember this older-brother, authority-figure pose. "What *about* Dad?" He pauses, knits his brow and looks like he is going to say something serious, then he says, "Well, I guess if he is goin' to go, he is goin' to go. Mom has constantly phoned me at work, complaining that he is dying. For God's sakes he's eighty. He's had a long life. *People die.* She should pull the plug, for God's sakes."

I don't want this to be part of my life. I hate dealing with him. Why did I have to drag myself all the way out here, when I could be home with David? If Dad died tonight, I could get home sooner. I try to get rid myself of my despair by picturing the steps I would go through to get back to California quickly. They are clinical and detached: I would be expected to attend the funeral, then the sit-in mourning. That would take about four days. When I am anxious, I start planning. It takes my mind off things.

I don't want to look weak in front of Harry. I try to sound mature. "But Harry, he is her husband. She loves him. They have been married for fifty-seven years." The adult part of me is back in control again. Suddenly another voice enters the conversation.

"Harry, how can you say that about your own father? What kind of person are you?"

The carpet has muffled my mother's approaching steps. She appears small and frail next to my brother's large, dense frame. What was a private, uncomfortable conversation between my brother and me now is public. I feel the room becoming smaller, but at the same time I feel smug that my brother is caught.

Harry's face reddens.

"I can't believe I heard you say this. I can't believe we raised a son who could talk this way."

He says nothing, just smacks his lips and looks down at the carpet.

She turns to me angrily. "I suppose you feel this way, too?"

"No, Mom, I don't. Really, I don't." But I'm not sure. Harry is right. Dad is old and death *is* inevitable. Mom would have me be selfish for thinking this way, but what would life be like for him or our family with his diminishing capacities?

She changes the subject, almost as if she didn't hear me. "Let's go. Dr. Arnstein says we can see Dad now. But they won't let us stay long."

She leads Harry and me down the corridor to the doorway of Dad's room. We put on blue masks with elastic bands in the back, and grab thin, flesh-colored latex gloves from a container that looks like a Kleenex box. The mask is uncomfortable on the bridge of my nose.

Dad is lying in the lemon-painted room with his mouth open. I can hear his audible wheezing. More tubes than yesterday assault his face, neck and arms. I don't know where my dad's body ends and technology begins. He looks smaller and grayer than he did yesterday. His skin is stretched across his body like rubber across a rim of a glass.

My mom leans over the edge of the bed and her face shows panic. Is he just asleep, or is he dead? She shakes him hard, like a rag doll. I see my brother flinch. When he was a teenager she got into fistfights with him in the kitchen. I was terrorized by what I saw.

Harry moves away to the far side of the bed. I'm taken aback that she is so heavy-handed with Dad's fragile body, and that my brother still fears her.

Dad would have said that Mom was just making sure he was okay. Did anyone else notice that over the decades how he'd changed slowly from a robust, opinionated, idealistic man to this?

Every day, we woke to the voice of Walter Cronkite and the blaring sound of KWOR radio, followed by a marching song of John Philip Sousa. Dad turned it up loud, as loud as his voice. He had a temper, and occasionally hauled off and hit me with his belt strap.

On Sundays, Aunt Helen and my cousins, Saul and Hermie, visited. Dad sat in the den with Uncle Abe, his brother-in-law, and Uncle Moe, his older brother, and smoked cigars. They got into heated arguments about Truman, the *Shvartzas* moving into Newark and taxes. My dad's booming voice shouted and argued his point above them all.

The year I went to college, around the time his mother died, he started to have panic attacks. He was having difficulties at his job. Although he had tenure and a good pension, he said his co-workers were trying to get him fired.

He seemed to recover, but he got quieter. Unapologetically, my mother slowly took over, while my dad receded into the newspaper. Years later he was diagnosed as having Parkinson's Disease.

I watch the strange man in bed and wonder: Is this man my father? Isn't my dad at home reading the newspaper in the den? The man in this bed must be someone else's father.

"Saul! Your son and daughter are here," says Mom in a near-hysterical voice. I have never seen my father look this pale and lifeless. His thin hair is matted in patches on his head, and a stubble of a beard grows on his face. I have never seen him so unkempt, and it frightens me.

"Wake up. SAUL." My mother starts shaking him again. Finally, he opens his small brown eyes and looks at each of us. "Oh, honey," Mom says with relief. "We thought you were...."

"I'm up, I'm up. I'm the best fighter in this place," he says, smiling weakly and closing his eyes again.

We stand around, awkward and silent. There is only one chair and my mother takes it. My brother and I stand on either side of the bed, looking at Dad.

I want to sit and snuggle against him, the way I did when we took Sunday afternoon naps together when I was seven. Mom frowns as I move toward the mattress. "No, Dear."

The four of us are together in the hospital room, silent. We have spent a lifetime of discomfort with each other. We have always been better in pairs, behind closed doors. Dad and me in the den, watching television, Mom and me in the kitchen, preparing a salad, Harry talking to Mom in her bedroom, while she is getting ready to go out. As a foursome we get into trouble quickly. A strong opinion, a disagreement, a dissent, and arguments and sides are quickly drawn, then flashes of anger and rage.

At that moment, a young nurse with a long blonde braid and freckles comes in. My memories evaporate. Her thin legs stretch out from under her short, white polyester uniform. She reminds me of a cheerleader from my high school. She couldn't be over twenty-five.

"So, Mr. Perlman, how are we this beautiful morning? Your family is here, I see. Maybe you'd like to leave while I do a little clean-up," she says to my mom cheerfully.

"We can stay," Mom says with an edge in her voice, as we move away from the bed.

"This is sort of messy, I'm not sure if you want to watch. It's not for people with weak stomachs." She turns to me and giggles.

She adjusts his respirator and takes the tube out of his throat. She suctions his mouth with a hand-held vacuum device, like something you would see in a dentist's office. Wouldn't that make a person want to gag, I wonder?

"This is a very sick man," the nurse addresses my mom. "His Parkinson's Disease is suppressing his immune system. Some of his functions seem to be shutting down. You can see his heart on this heart monitor." She points to a beeping metal monitor and a line flowing across the screen. "It's unstable now. You probably should leave." She smiles but urges us with her body language.

My mother leans over my dad's bed and kisses him on the forehead. I squeeze his hand. Harry imitates me.

The three of us, led by my mother, shuffle out in to the white linoleum corridor.

My father no longer feels as if he belongs to me, but like a lifeless soul kept alive to please my mother.

5

While my dad slowly deteriorated, when Mom and I could sit no longer, and the night nurse was finally on the edge of her patience, so we fled again and again to the shopping malls that dotted Northern New Jersey. "Shopping is to New Jersey what skiing is to Vermont," I told my mom jokingly. She smiled at me.

We shopped as a refuge: a kaleidoscope of colorful new spring clothes and gaggles of sauntering groups of youthful people in the mall in contrast to the cool linoleum-lined hallways, lemon-colored walls and airless rooms of the hospital. The rhythm of our visits took on a life of its own through the bitterly cold winter of 1992 and the spring of 1993.

My dad lay in bed as organ after organ slowly deteriorated, but my mother never lost hope. She held his hand, looked into his cloudy eyes and pleaded, "You gotta fight Saul, you gotta fight." I hated my mother's willfulness. I was torn between letting my dad go and supporting my mom's desire to have him whole again.

Spring came late that year. I flew in every four weeks and stayed for long weekends. Mom and I sat on either side of Dad's bed watching CNN, which blared day and night. The television, mounted high above our heads on the opposite wall, was our only connection to a gray, icy world that was melting into spring slush.

"I just didn't have time to plant the daffodils near the kitchen window this spring," my mother said absentmindedly. She always got so excited when she saw their heads break through the hard soil, so I wondered if she was losing hope, too.

The nurses and orderlies quietly entered, peered momentarily up at the screen with vague interest, and then turned toward my dad to clean out his respirator, or the tube that went down his throat into his stomach or the one attached to his penis, or to just wash him down with a damp cloth. He complied and smiled, too weak to talk.

We saw images of people in Florida still recovering from Hurricane Andrew's wrath from late autumn of the year before. At least their hope was renewed by actions and rebuilding, unlike our unspoken waning hope and endless waiting.

Mom gossiped with me about Aunt Helen and Uncle Abe and their decision to move from Newark to St. Petersburg several years before. There were images on the TV screen of ice and snow burying Manhattan to Maryland with twenty-degree temperatures and wind chill factors of minus ten.

Stiff-faced George Bush and glib Bill Clinton postured on platforms in thawing Midwestern cities, positioning themselves for the 1994 election.

But the real excitement during those months at the hospital was the unexpected labor of singer Whitney Houston, who was rushed by a helicopter that whisked her from her plush condo in Manhattan to the roof of St. Barnabas, where she delivered a baby boy.

My mother left my dad's bedside briefly to join in the gossip at the nurse's station with the women who had crept up to the maternity ward to see Whitney's six-pound baby. The hospital people were rapidly becoming Mom's family. I joined in the gossip and intrigue, happy that Mom was occupied with something other than illness for the moment.

One day, she told me that she attended a lecture in the main auditorium of the hospital while Dad slept. Whereas other families seemed stiff and awkward in the linoleum halls, Mom settled right into her role as Dad's caretaker. Perhaps this place seemed familiar from Mom's nurse's training days.

The hospital my dad was dying in, had been dying inch by inch over the last eight months, was a place I detested.

Because I hated the airless corridors, the glaring ceiling florescent lights, the Lysol-smelling bathrooms with the machines that clicked off metered-out pieces of paper towels, I didn't want to become a part of it as Mom was doing. I acted like a stranger to it, but I had to admit the place was getting comfortable.

It was my mother, measuring out her days sitting by my father's bedside, who became my guide. I borrowed her eyes to appreciate the winter sunset through the hospital windows. We sat in silence on the side of the bed while Dad dozed, each holding one of his hands. Outside, mauve turned to Persian blue, and then to black. The trunks of the bare oaks were framed against the night sky.

She put her index finger to her lips and we tiptoed out, trying not to wake Dad. She led me down the empty night corridors and through the swinging doors of the service elevator. Mom showed me every nook and cranny of that small city of a hospital, and she knew practically everyone who worked there. That's how I learned to find my way from the ICU by a the short cut, and out the emergency room exit without anyone stopping me.

Several times a day, Dad scribbled cramped little messages on a large legal pad of paper, slowly and painfully. "I liked the chocolate pudding today," or "Let the nurse know that I need to be washed." Every morning Mom was there by nine to shave him and comb his hair. One morning when I arrived he was wide-awake and smiling. Some color had come back into his face. He had carefully composed several sentences to show me: "Honey, I saw a program late last night about a psychologist. I couldn't sleep, so I watched. Now, I understand everything." His eyes began to tear. He wrote very slowly. "I always wondered about those book titles on your shelves. Now I understand what you are learning."

For a second, an old connection sparked. I felt hopeful. Did he finally see me? I wanted so badly for my dad to *see* me. In his eyes, I felt like a child. He was always the grown-up. I couldn't influence him in any way, and finally that is what drove me away, drove me to join the Peace Corps in Africa, to live with a non-Jewish man. "Why does she want to humiliate us so? Why is she ruining her life?" he questioned. When I heard this I felt so ashamed and misunderstood.

One day years ago, I called to tell him that I was looking for another job.

After a long pause, he asked, "But Honey, I thought you had a job!"

"I *do*, Dad." I tried to hide the impatience in my voice.

"Well, if you have a job, why do you want another?"

His world was the Depression and then, finally, after several menial jobs when good work wasn't given to Jews, he did government work for forty years. It was inconceivable to him that you should change jobs, unless, of course, you were fired.

So I told myself that he was not capable of showing love; that helped for many years to create some soft tissue over the deep wound.

But now, I thought, perhaps there would be an opening into which I could pour all my missed opportunities and dreams. We could really connect, now before it was too late. We could swim into the deep lagoon, where the waters were warm and clear. A place I could go back to in my mind after he was gone. A place where I was assured that he really loved me all along, but couldn't express it. I would happily accept that for just one moment of recognition from him.

"I was thinking about how you looked in high school. You are beautiful, my dear. How is your car running?"

I laughed. The moment slipped away again. Whenever there was some stickiness between us, he would ask about my car. Maybe it was just a safe topic, or maybe, if my car was running well, then he felt I was able to take care of myself. There are just some things you never really figure out.

"Dad, you'll get better soon. Then you can come home and all the newspapers that you read will be waiting for you. Mom and I piled them up each day — three of the New York dailies, two of the Newark papers, and the Jewish news," I lied.

Then I said "Dad? Remember the time that you, Mom, David and I were driving down to Monterey?"

He found his voice from deep inside. It was rasping and halting. "Yes, I loved that trip. I shall always remember it." He smiled and his cloudy brown eyes softened at the memory.

"Do you remember when I told you about a movie I saw where the two soldiers make a vow that if either of them gets killed, they will come back and leave a sign for the other that they are okay on the other side?"

"Yes, Honey, I do," he said. "And do you remember what I told you? I said that if I am able wherever I am, I will do that for you and more. And I will let you know that I arrived safely."

We both laughed at the same time at the image of him arriving safely, as if he were driving his big Buick Regal up to heaven. I felt better.

"You know, Honey," he said, "I don't plan on going anywhere just yet. I asked God to let me live just one more year to see your book published, and to celebrate our fifty-eighth wedding anniversary. That will be one year more than my mother and father were married."

At that moment, I knew he would make it, too.

When I was seven, my dad said that I would be a famous writer some day. I was writing poems and stories and he taught me how to type them up on his little portable Underwood typewriter. It was his dream. I wanted to be an artist.

On Sunday afternoons when I was in junior high school, he would take out his beat-up Stradivarius violin and serenade us.

"It is a rare person that can combine their vocation and avocation," he told me. That stuck in my mind when career day arrived at school. Parents came to talk about their jobs. The boys could choose to be doctors, lawyers, accountants, dentists, firemen or other things. The girls had only three choices: nursing ("One nurse is enough in this family!" said Mom), teaching or being a librarian. I loved to read, so I traipsed along after the other girls who were to be future librarians of America.

The school librarian, Mrs. Braithewaite, taught us the Dewey Decimal System and then gave us a gurney of books and told us to help them "find their little homes again." In the stacks, I got tired of all the numbers and decimals, so I found new little homes for the books and I was done in no time. I announced my untimely accomplishment to Mrs. Braithewaite, found my coat and walked home.

Early the next morning, she called my mother. "I don't think your girl has the aptitude for library science," she said. "Perhaps she should be a teacher."

My mother related this to me and added, "First you'll go to college. Then you'll get married to a doctor. Besides, you can always find a job as a teacher. Something to fall back on." My future was settled. I didn't really like the plan, but I had thought of nothing on my own to take its place. Besides, the future seemed pretty far off to me.

I couldn't understand why getting into college was more important than being popular (without getting pregnant) with the boys. Getting into college required studying, a solitary activity. Being popular was a far easier thing for me.

When I was a junior in high school, I worked at Altman's during Christmas vacation. I wanted my own money to buy gifts. One night, when my dad came by to pick me up after work, I dragged myself, exhausted, into the passenger seat. I had spent a long, hard day of hauling clothes back from the fitting rooms. I tried as hard as I could to put them back on hangers faster than the women could try them on and drop them on the floor.

"Dad, is this what grown-ups do for a living?" I asked.

There was a pause, then he said softly, "That's what they do, Honey, if they don't have a college education."

My efforts at popularity won out over my struggle to be smart. When it came time to graduate high school and go away to college, I stayed home and went to Rutgers, Newark. This was my first failure in life — a microcosm of what my life could be like if I got pregnant by mistake, couldn't find a suitable career, or worst yet, couldn't drum up the right husband. It was a taste of the default position in my potential-not-yet-lived-life.

It only cost two hundred dollars a year to matriculate at Rutgers, and it was ten miles away from home. It was a melting pot of poor Italians, Jews, blacks and new arrivals on our shining shores. A cross-section of humanity sat in the crowded classes. The emphasis was on getting in and getting out with an undergraduate degree while working a day job. Worst of all, the college was in the ghetto of Newark. In order to register for the right classes, you had to camp at the front door of the registrars and be near the front of the line when the door of the college opened.

I tried to stay out of trouble with my mother and keep a low profile. Mom and Dad's routines were predictable: get up, go to work, come home, eat supper, watch television and go to bed. "We don't have enough money to send both you and Harry away to school," my mother complained. "Besides, your father doesn't believe that you need a college education. Why waste money when you'll just get married?" she said. Clearly, she was more hopeful than I.

I needed a vision. Out of desperation, I devised a plan. I sent applications to schools hundred of miles away, hoping that if I got in, my parents would be flattered to know I really was smart. Maybe I'd get a scholarship, maybe I'd get lucky. They would find a way to send me.

When Dad saw me filling out college applications, he got panicky. "If you insist on filling out these applications, I don't want you going more then three hundred miles away. I want to be able to drive there and visit you."

"Can't you hop on a plane?" I asked.

"I don't like to fly," he said. I was surprised at this admission of a weakness.

"Why can't you learn from my experience? Stay home!" Mom said.

So I made a concession. We looked at a map and drew a 300-mile circumference with our town in the center. From there I began researching schools that were around the farthest point from the center.

Skidmore was one of them. One Saturday we went up for an interview and later came the feedback, via the registrar that I was, "a very gregarious girl." I knew what that word meant because it was on my Graduate Record Exams. What an uproar at my house when I got in.

My mother told all her friends that I got into a "seven sister school." I was embarrassed for her. At best, Skidmore was a seven sister wannabe.

So early in September 1963, I packed up my bicycle, books and clothes and was driven to Skidmore College by my proud mother and father, who miraculously came up with the money to send me. My dad made me promise him to repay the tuition once I graduated and got a job. I would have signed anything to leave. Later he showed the piece of paper to my new husband and asked him to take over the unpaid loan.

What a disappointment to find the dorm was an old mansion on Skidmore Campus in the run down town of Saratoga. We walked up the four flights of stairs and found my garret room with two beds and two desks jammed into a space no bigger than a closet.

My roommate, Karen, a transfer student, was a priggish Catholic girl from Bernardsville, a posh town northwest of Maplewood, with lots of money. Her dad was the president of a national girdle company.

You would think that life would immediately get better having logged in so many hours fantasizing about running away from home. It did not. It got worse.

My roommate took an immediate dislike to me. Maybe I still had that afterbirth on me that kids have who haven't been around, and new kids know it.

She moved out within the first semester, and I had the attic room all to myself. I became friendly with the girl across the hall. She was quiet and sensitive. She wrote poetry and slept in the hallway when her roommate kicked her out because she was snoring. Abby didn't seem to mind. On school break, I went to visit her at her home in Chatham. She lived in a huge house set back from the street by a lawn that had to be mowed by a man sitting on top of a mechanical lawn mover. The amazing thing was when I met her tabby cat, Heloise, a reflective little soul, it could have been Abby herself. "The newsboy hit my cat in the head with the paper one morning, so she sits and faces the wall most of the day," she said.

Abby introduced me to Ellen, who lived downstairs. Ellen was a tall blonde with no hips. She was my female ideal of what a woman should look like, and she had her own horse. Her dad was a head honcho at Dartmouth, and although she wasn't rich, by any means, she had her own car. At the end of the school year, when girls were contemplating whom they wanted to room with in their senior year, Ellen, out of the clear blue, asked me. I was flabbergasted, but Ellen took me under her wing and took me up to Dartmouth on weekends, taught me how to dress (WASP style), and ski, and gave me a crash course on etiquette in New England. Things like yes means no, don't say what you mean, be polite at all costs, give backhanded compliments and never raise your voice. She was the one who introduced me to my first husband.

I decided to get serious, go to college and get an apartment in Manhattan with my girlfriend Beatrice after I graduated.

"What are you gonna do when you graduate college?" Mom asked one day.

"Beatrice and I are going to share an apartment in Manhattan."

"And how do you plan to pay for it?"

"I'll get a job, I suppose. "

"Over my dead body. No daughter of mine is going to slut around Manhattan. She can't learn by someone else's experience! You'll live at home, where we can meet the men who want to court you!" she screamed. "Saul, Saul, come here and hear this! I need this like a *loch in kop* (hole in the head)!"

"But what if I can't find someone to marry after a few years?" I begged.

"By then, you'll be used goods, then you can take your apartment in Manhattan with Beatrice," she snorted.

I couldn't believe my ears. I couldn't accept this. She always said that when I reached twenty-one, I was on my own, and I believed her. Now she was saying something entirely different. Even after I was grown up, my mother still had plans for me on how to live my life.

So it was a gift from God that I found the only Jewish boy at Dartmouth, who also had an overbearing mother and the same desire to escape the East Coast.

We pored over a map of the United States and let our fingers land on the farthest place from Maplewood, New Jersey. It was LaPush, Washington.

In June 1965 we graduated college, got married, bought a red Corvair and waved good-bye to my parents, who stood on the steps of 31 Magnolia Avenue. What a moment!

I was a success at the age of nineteen! I had escaped, un-impregnated, not an embarrassment to my family, at least not yet.

It's funny how your life takes shape from these moments strung together like cultured pearls on a necklace. Each event is unremarkable in itself. Admiring friends can step back and be dazzled by the necklace, but only you know what it took to make it.

What could this man in front of me in the hospital bed know of my struggle to stand on my own two feet? What could I know about his struggle now?

I wanted to ask him if he was afraid. I wanted to ask him how he felt lying there day after day, but I couldn't form the sentences to start the conversation. I felt frozen. I felt like I was watching a sad Disney movie of someone else's daughter and her father.

Many years and many moves later, when I had begun my doctoral program, my dad and mom visited me in Amherst,

Massachusetts. I had just driven across the country from San Francisco and found an apartment to live in several miles from campus. My parents were sitting at the newly purchased second-hand kitchen table. It was my third day there. Classes hadn't begun. This definitely was not what I had anticipated my living arrangements to be. Instead of Cape Cod-like cottages dotting an elm tree-lined street, large concrete and glass buildings rose out of the cornfields. Buses shuttled back and forth to low-lying new brick apartment complexes as students rushed from class to class.

I sat in the kitchen of my place, shared with an Asian woman who answered my ad, and cried to my parents about how I missed California. Outside the windows, the oaks were losing their leaves.

"After all this, you're still not happy!" Dad yelled and threw up his hands in exasperation. "After we spent all this money!" His eyes became small and hard. He put his head in his hands and let out a sigh.

"Oh, Dad it's not that. It's just all so new. I miss my old life." I cried because I felt that one chapter was ending and a new and unfamiliar one was beginning. It was overwhelming for me, and I felt unseen and misunderstood.

Dad turned toward my mother. "Sarah, explain this to me. I don't understand her." He pushed back his chair and stood up. The chair slid across the polished bare wood floor and crashed against the wall. He stomped out of the building, and I saw him in the yard below staring off into the Berkshire Hills.

In the silence of the kitchen, with my books and clothes still in boxes lining the wall, Mom and I looked at one another. "You shouldn't upset your father like that," she scolded.

"I'm sorry, I'm sorry, I'm sorry," I repeated softly to her, feeling hopeless.

So no one could delve into the rich loamy soil of sadness or loss in my family. Maybe it was because we had a legacy of sadness, but I know that some time way before then I decided never to share my softer feelings. To never allow them to see me as weak or to humiliate me. And I wasn't sure enough in myself to see that in my vulnerability lay my strength. Now in the hospital, the magnitude of the fact that my father could die was never mentioned. It was too distasteful.

I wondered if my belief in his recovery was all that it really took. That if I had strong faith, he could defy the doctors, even at the age of eighty, and walk out of the hospital. Or was this feeling about my father's invincibility, the same one I had as a child, a naive faith that had never been tested? If I prayed hard enough, if I wanted it enough, would God hear me? I wasn't sure anymore.

Just before Easter in my fourth grade class at my new school, an oversized popcorn and caramel bunny appeared on Miss Auner's desk in front of the room. It was wrapped in cellophane and tied with a huge pink satin ribbon. I daydreamed about how it would taste all gooey and crunchy. Mysteriously, it remained on her desk in front of the room for several days before she finally announced, "On Friday, we'll draw numbers. Whoever gets the winning one wins the popcorn bunny."

Unbeknownst to anyone, I had secretly been testing God for several months. Certainly, God could give me a sign now. If we really were the Chosen People, I needed to be sure that my own special God was watching over me in this new school.

I had been devising small tests of God, to see if I had his attention. If Beth Rosenhauser was standing at the corner waiting to walk me to school, or if Joanie Nottingham was not in gym class that day, I knew then that God was helping me. Winning the popcorn bunny would be the real test.

So that night and for every night that week, I prayed non-stop to God for that bunny. I repeated the same prayer over and over again:

"Dear God, please let me win the popcorn bunny. Dear God, please let me win the popcorn bunny."

On Friday morning, none of the kids could sit still. Just before lunchtime, Miss Auner cut pieces of paper into little strips and put numbers from one to thirty on them. Then she asked Howard Kempler to fold the strips and put them into his baseball cap. As he walked around the room and offered his cap to each of us, my prayer was going strong.

I picked a slip with a number out of the hat and opened it. The nights of not sleeping and the tension had gotten to me. I was in a daze.

Once we all had our numbers. Miss Auner said, "Who has seven? That's the winning number."

I let out a gasp. The bunny was mine. She handed it to me with a big smile.

We were all crowded by the door, when Ralph Santana, a skinny Italian kid, leaned over to me. "How did you win the bunny?" he asked in awe.

Everyone stopped talking. All eyes were on me. "I prayed to God," I said.

In that moment, I knew I had said the wrong thing. The kids rolled their eyes and giggled.

After school, I trudged home alone, lugging the bunny. It must have weighed a good seven pounds. Once I got into the empty house, I tore open the cellophane and bit into the bunny. It tasted dry and stale, and I felt a deep disappointment that maybe this was not what I had really wanted.

I didn't give up, although I was distressed. I needed God. Clearly He didn't need me.

At twenty-one, I was still at it. I begged God to make my

pregnancy test negative after having sex outside of marriage with Jeff. My own special God came through, again.

So here I was now, praying once again about my father, waiting for God to hear me. Maybe God was hearing me, but Dad had stopped talking. He seemed to be working on something deeply internal, as if he were unraveling all the years of detail, data, facts, scrutiny, and paranoia he had accumulated as a Special Agent of the Internal Revenue Service.

Frequently, I wondered, why is he continuing to remain alive? Was it the force of my mother that was holding him here? Was she unraveling, too?

I caught glimpses of a frightened little girl hiding behind mom's fierce self-reliance.

Early one morning, I was admiring a white wool shawl with a popcorn stitch she had crocheted before dad took ill. "I'll make you one," she said spontaneously and pulled some leftover beige wool out of her cloth brocade crochet bag. "But I don't have enough wool."

"Let's go to the yarn store and get some more today. On the way to the hospital," I suggested. I knew it was a purely selfish whim on my part.

"No, they won't have it, she said. "Let's not go."

I suddenly felt annoyed at her. Here she offered something, and then took it back. "What is it?" I said in a familiar, resistant tone of voice. In a flash we were on the verge of bursting into the white heat of our rage at each other — passions from earlier times that could flare up at a moment's notice.

"I just feel like everything is going against me now. I just don't have the strength. I don't feel that I can do anything anymore. It's self-confidence — my self confidence is shot."

"Oh, Mom." I knew that this dying was breaking her open too, regardless of the toughness she showed the world. Then I remembered that it had always been this way with my mom.

In her five-foot frame, she was David to the Goliath world that thwarted her: getting a job in the 1950's when only women who had to worked, securing a credit card when women could only get credit in their husbands' names.

In that moment, I wanted to give my mother everything she never got in life. I wanted to take her in my arms and tell her everything was going to go back to the way it was: normal, pleasant and predictable. But I couldn't. All I could say was, "Mom, it's okay. We don't have to go there. I understand."

It was only while we sat hour after hour at Dad's bedside that Mom began to talk about Dad's nervous breakdown, a secret she had kept hidden from me.

"It happened the year you went to college. You were so busy, I didn't want to disturb you," she told me. "Nothing worked. All the doctors and all the medication didn't help. Finally, I pleaded to him on my knees. 'Saul, Saul, I need you. What will happen to me if you leave me?' It was only then that he snapped out of it."

Why didn't she tell me earlier? Was she ashamed? Or was this the thing she feared the most — not illness, not death, but mental incapacitation? In light of Dad's physical decline, I couldn't take in what she was telling me.

In Dad's eyes, I began to see an unraveling, like a tightly wound ball of yarn unwinding. In the unraveling, I could almost see the vague indentations of the layers beneath, no longer hidden from view.

Did he know that he was dying? Like every other collusion in their marriage, they both must have known, but didn't talk about it. Mom wanted Dad to live, and he was doing his best for her.

They had their secret language based on a half-century of feeling each other's presence, a closeness, knowing each other's touch and odors — from work, from lovemaking, from coming in from the yard after an afternoon of raking leaves.

I had wanted that so badly for myself in a relationship, before I met David. My jealousy was palpable when I saw it between them. Now I could understand it as a rare bonding, because I was growing into the same place with David. After years of trying to change each other, we began cultivating the softer moments, and so there were more of those cherished times together. He grew into my confidante and my teacher over the last several years. I trusted him.

I wanted Dad to live for her. I wanted her to have him and never have to give up the mysterious way they sensed each other's moods and thoughts — like the way the air shifts in a meadow and the animals raise their heads, or the way the mountain casts a shadow over the valley beneath my house — imperceptible movements in the late afternoon. I wanted her to have that together with him, forever, maybe because it made me feel safe, too.

One morning, Mr. Feinstein, the lawyer came to Dad's hospital room. "I want you to sign this with Dad and me," Mom said. Mr. Feinstein guided Dad's hand. "Dad and I agreed that you should be the co-executor of the will with Harry." It was settled then. I felt something in my relationship with my mom shift into place. I thought that she finally felt comfortable with me and trusted me to take care of her.

Later that day she said, "I have something else for you. I've been saving it."

We were sitting in the tiny kitchen sharing some tea and butter cookies as we had done so many other times in our lives. She moved close and took my hand.

"Honey, I want you to have these two diamonds. I'm giving them to you without Harry knowing, because I want you to pass them on to Harry's daughter and not let them get into Roberta's hands. These diamonds were brought over from Russia by my grandmother. She sewed them into the hem of her coat on her passage over and used them for collateral many times. I went with her sometimes to pawn them in the winter to get money to fix up a rundown delicatessen. In the summer, when the business was doing well, I would go with her and get them back out of hock. She was clutching them when they found her on the bus going up to Kiamesha Lake to open High View Hotel for the summer tourists. It was the first of two heart attacks that killed her."

She placed a wedding band with two sparkling stones in my hand.

"Keep them safe," she said.

That night I got a call from my brother. "I heard that Mr. Feinstein paid you all a visit," he said. "I can't believe you made Mom and Dad sign those papers. That I have to share in this with you."

"I was as surprised as you are," I defended myself. "I didn't know it was happening until she announced it to me."

"You'll be sorry for this," he said. His voice chilled me.

6

I wouldn't have gone home that afternoon if I had another place to go. By now, all the other fifth grade girls were at the Girl Scout meeting in the church basement. The windows were high up with metal bars and they made me claustrophobic. I didn't want to go back there.

I started the long trek up tree-lined Summit Avenue. This time of year the air was getting crisper, and it pierced my nostrils as I climbed the hill.

Loneliness swelled inside me. I turned the corner to Magnolia Avenue and looked down the street to my empty house. Other porch lights were coming on now, but my house looked empty and locked up in the December dusk.

I walked up the driveway and searched for my key. It felt cold against the palm of my hand in the pocket of my red woolen jacket. Absentmindedly, I bent down to pet Fluffy, the big white Persian cat that lived on the other side of the driveway.

I didn't want to go inside just yet. It was cold and dark inside, and all the "Twilight Zone" television episodes came to my mind when I thought of opening the back door with my key. So I followed Fluffy to the back stairs of the Hamiltons' house next door.

Out poked a little paw from under the steps. Then another one. Four kittens scampered out and up the stairs to greet me. They all looked like Fluffy and A.T., her daughter. I unzipped my jacket and slid them all inside. They stepped all over one another and started purring almost in unison.

I had begged Dad for a kitten many times. It was the first item on my birthday list, but I always ended up disappointed. "We work, and there is no one to take care of it," he said.

Just then A.T. came around the corner, up the stairs, and brushed against me. I remember Mrs. Hamilton telling me that A.T. got her name from her short tail because when she was a kitten someone slammed it in the refrigerator door by accident. A.T. stood for afterthought.

I sat outside in the dark, waiting for my mom to come home. The air smelled pungent from burning leaves, and the kittens settled into my pockets. I made believe that I was their pussy-cat mother, and I started to feel reassured. Maybe my mother would come home early. I listened for the sound of the funny way her heels clicked in double time when she walked on the asphalt toward the house.

The kittens heard Mrs. Hamilton coming before I did. I could feel them shifting their weight under my jacket and crawling over one another for the light opening inside the dark warmth. The largest one's head came out first and his half-closed eyes opened and paused to look directly into mine.

The kitchen door opened abruptly behind me. I could feel the rush of air, and the warm smells of food filled my nostrils: fried chicken, mashed potatoes and the lingering richness of onions fried in butter. "Oh, hello, Dear. I didn't know you were here." Mrs. Hamilton wiped her hands on her apron and then shivered in the cold. The kittens quickly scrambled out of my jacket and ran inside. My belly felt empty from the hole the kittens had left behind.

A mixture of shame and humiliation mingled in me as I huddled on her gray wooden porch steps, trying to get up casually. "Well, I guess I should be going. I'd better do my homework," I offered. Better to save face, act like I had something more important to do. Who needs her stupid cats!

Slowly, I made my way across the black asphalt that was our driveway.

I felt a twinge of fear as I walked up the wooden stairs. Resentment as they groaned under my feet from the ice between the cracks. I was the only kid in school who wore a key around her neck. Three days a week when I had gym, I hid the key in my pocket because I didn't want the kids to see it and tease me, or worse, steal it from me.

Sherry Scher, Beverly Nonnen, and Elaine Stein didn't have to open their doors. I knew that they had mothers who would hear their knock, open the door to a warm house, settle them into a kitchen chair and treat them to hot chocolate or milk and homemade cookies.

I was a hostage in a big dark house. I sat at the kitchen table with my coat on. The kitchen wall clock ticked off each second like an hour. The darkness was like an intruder who pervaded our house, beckoning me further into its interior.

What price would I pay if I entered the living room to turn on the lamps? What terror would I feel if I ran into the den and turned on the television? What horror would I see if I rushed into the dining room to turn up the thermostat? Upstairs in my dark bedroom, I could get my books, but if I left the kitchen and then returned, the intruder might be there — hiding in the foyer or blocking my escape out the back door.

I heard a sound upstairs, and it sent shivers through my body. A car drove by, but it didn't stop in our driveway. I sat very still biting my nails as I listened to the clock tick, and the sound of my own breath, as I tried to keep the intruder at bay. Suddenly, there were heavy footsteps on the porch stairs, laughter, the sound of keys jiggling and a turn in the lock.

I heard my big brother's voice. "Hey, why is it so dark in here?" He opened the door, and it broke the stillness and sent a chill of brittle air into the room.

I froze. He ignored me as he took off his winter coat and threw it on the chair. His dense, thirteen-year-old body was a mystery to me. He smelled rancid and pungent and dirty.

Two more boys his age tumbled into the kitchen, ignoring me. They wore heavy cloth jackets and blue jeans. Greg had red straight hair and wide blue eyes. My dad said that he was an Irish Potato kid. His dad was a fireman and had to feed six children.

Danny unzipped his coat. He had dark skin and long black hair. Mom suspected that although he came from a devout Catholic family, he had some black blood. "I don't know how Mrs. Hall gave birth to a kid that looked like that," she had said.

I got up, turned my back to them, and started walking into the den. I knew Greg and Danny. I didn't want to be near them. I felt overwhelmed and invaded now, but no longer scared. I was relieved to have company, in a way. I turned on the light in the den, took off my coat, and turned on channel thirteen to see if *American Bandstand* was still on.

I didn't notice when the door opened. I was leaning on my side with my coat thrown down beside me. I looked up at them with curiosity and turned back to the screen. They stood over me, hesitatingly.

"What do you want?" I asked irritably. I could smell Greg's jacket and the grease on Danny's hair. I had been keeping my feet flat on the floor, but now I pulled them up to my chest and made my body into a ball.

"What *is* it?" I insisted. Suddenly, I sensed their purpose, not in words, but in animal fear. I bolted up, but Danny grabbed me.

Greg and Danny were upon me. I didn't fully comprehend what was happening, but I felt their will, and I knew they had done this before. While Greg grabbed and held my feet, Danny fumbled with his pants. I tried to fight.

"Let me go! Let me go!" I screamed.

Greg had pinned me down by pressing my arms against the back of the couch.

"You're hurting me! Get off me!"

"Help me!" I let out a startled cry. For a second Danny's eyes met mine.

"Danny, I hear someone coming," Greg said.

Little crying sounds kept coming out of my mouth, little animal sounds. I couldn't hold them back. Danny crushed my face sideways into the cushion. I tasted the salty sweat of his palm as he pushed himself up off the couch.

"Someone's coming," Greg warned again. "Let's get out of here."

Greg released his grip on me. They hurriedly ran out of the house. I overheard Danny saying to Greg outside in the driveway, "How old is she?"

I remained still and frightened. My bones ached, my face burned and there was a strange odor on my skin. Shame washed over me. It grew dark. I sobbed quietly until I heard my mother's voice as the key turned in the lock. My father was right behind her.

"Why is it so cold and dark in here? Turn on some lights!" My mother's voice was strident and demanding.

Only then did I get up and walk into the kitchen. Now unafraid, I swept my tears away with the cuff of my coat and turned the lights on. My hand did not feel like it belonged to my body.

"Where's Harry?" she asked.

"I don't know." I tried to sound casual. Did she see my flushed face, or sense anything abnormal?

She ran upstairs with urgency. I heard the bathroom toilet flush. Then she came downstairs and began to throw supper together. I could hear the banging of the saucepan and the frying pan on the top of the gas stove.

My dad's pace was slower. It seemed like the weight of the day settled onto him as he took his evening newspapers and walked into the den to read. "How was school?" he asked suddenly.

"Okay," I said evenly. He couldn't help me.

That evening, supper was a rude affair and a rush job of frozen tater tots and burnt minute steaks. My dad silently stuffed food down his mouth like a hungry animal, and my mother asked, "More, Saul? More, Saul?," shoving the food platter in front of his face before he was half done.

My brother arrived moments before dinner. I felt so ashamed seeing him. Did he know? Where had he been?

"I can't believe we are having frozen food," he complained. "What happened to real French fries and burgers in this house? Will we ever get real home cooking again?"

Mom ignored him. "Why are you so quiet?" she asked suddenly, turning to me. I sat paralyzed and didn't reply.

Harry sat with his head bent over his plate as he shoveled his food down. I couldn't see his eyes. I didn't want him to see mine.

Much later, as I got ready for bed, Mom came in and sat down on the edge of my bed. She wanted to talk about her day at work. "The black kids at the school sometimes don't eat breakfast, so about eleven they get very sleepy," she told me. "The principal doesn't want to give them the leftover milk, but I think the school district should. We would throw it out anyway."

I thought about my life at school compared to the world she traveled to as a nurse in a ghetto school. It seemed so far away, different, and it scared me.

"Did you walk to school with Beth this morning?" she asked.

"No, she had left before I got there," I said.

"Don't worry, you'll make more friends." Then she put her hand under my pajama top and rubbed my back, and soon her soothing voice lulled me to sleep.

Suddenly, I awoke to pressure over my mouth. I shook my head violently. I looked up wide-eyed and wild. The house was still. I didn't know if I had dreamed what had happened that afternoon or not. The clock radio on the desk showed it was three in the morning. I lay there awake until dawn.

7

Mom's voice sounds panicky over the phone.

"Dear, Dad has taken another turn for the worst. He has septicemia again," she says. "He's asking for you. You must come now! Dr. Arnstein says it looks bad. This may be the last time, Dear." Yet another close call, so many close calls. I am emotionally drained at this point.

If she is panicking, shouldn't I be? She has always been the strong one. I hear my mother's silent questioning: "What will I do if he goes? Why aren't you here to help me?" I feel spent and helpless.

"You plan on coming?" She asks this like a question, but it is a demand.

"It depends if I can get a reservation," I hedge. It's my reluctant way to appease her and my guilt. Perhaps by morning she will feel differently.

"He *is* your father!"

"I *know* he is my father, Ma!"

Then there is silence on the line. The white rage is boiling under the surface again.

I want Dad to recover. I want Dad to have peace. But I can't live my life with all these interruptions. I can't run my business and run back and forth to the East Coast at the same time.

I fight back. I stand by my sink, talking to her and dicing carrots to put into a casserole for dinner. The knife comes down quicker and harder.

I feel like I have a zipper up the front of my body and anyone in my family can unzip me at anytime and take whatever they want. Stuff the anger inside. Just run, and do, and go, and drop dead from sacrifice. I see now what is valued in my family is sacrificing your own unique gifts to rescue and comfort and console others. It is a legacy handed down from mother to daughter. Everyone will cluck their tongues and shake their heads and say what a good daughter I was.

No! I fight inside myself. People die. Parents die. Look at him! I wanted to shout through the phone at her. He's on a respirator. He hasn't left his bed in eight months. He defecates, breathes and eats though tubes that must be cleaned several times a day. You have a living corpse. Are you going to sit with him until he rots from the inside out? And what then? Could you go on without him?

And then there will just be me and Harry. I will be alone and unprotected again.

I feel I am fighting an undertow that wants to sweep me out to sea. It is so hard to pull back from my life here three thousand miles away. I have worked so hard to stand on my own two feet and make a living. I chose independence: marriage, but separate incomes and no children to slow me down.

I am a product of my time. I thought I was a good feminist. I thought I could have it all: a lucrative career, a successful husband, a family. But no one ever really lives by her own agenda. I too was hypnotized by our time: there was a price to pay. There were trade-offs no one told me about. How much of the politics of the zeitgeist co-ops us? In trying not to overvalue men and or plead for their acceptance and approval, I remained alone and single and childless. I concentrated on my career. I told myself that this was what was really important. I bought the idea that I had to become the right kind of person for the right person to come along. He did after a while but in the final wash, wasn't I a victim of a much large picture, after all? What would I have done if I hadn't been swept up in 'sixties activism and 'seventies feminism? Could I then have followed that small, still voice inside? Would I have even heard it?

I worry about my clients. I will have to cancel on them if I go back East again. I can't let this business I have built against all odds just deteriorate.

"I will call you back in the morning. I'll call the airlines now," I say.

"Thank you, Dear. See you tomorrow." Her voice has soften, but I am still uncertain of my decision.

I pick up the phone and dial my brother. I want a familiar voice, someone to commiserate with. I'm surprised to hear his voice right after the first ring. I tell him what has just happened. I feel ashamed that my voice, relating my conversation with Mom sounds so plaintive.

"Yep," he says and then there is a characteristic long pause. Finally, he answers my plea for empathy. "I've been getting calls like that for the last four months. Tomorrow, when Dad stabilizes, she'll be okay again." Then he gives a funny gurgling sound, like a giggle with his hand over his mouth. I don't know what to make of it.

"Or maybe he won't this time."

"Thanks, Harry. You are a help!" I feel my patience being tested. Does he know he was toying with my emotions? Suddenly, I want to get off the phone.

"Well you certainly screwed me by making Mom put you as co-executor of the will," he suddenly shouts.

There is an ocean of silence between us.

I don't want to fight but I want to defend myself.

"So, are you going BACK?" he shouts.

"Yes," I answer quietly. My anger flares. I decide to go. The choice comes from somewhere deep inside me. Am I so obsessed with beating out my brother at all costs? No — it isn't about my brother. No matter what my mother asks, I will do it out of love for her.

"Give my love to Roberta and Francine, I've got to go." I hang up, glad to be off the line. I dial the airlines and book a flight out the next day.

I wait until David and I are lying in bed that night to tell him. "Oh, no!" He moans. "How long will you be away this time?"

His response upsets me. I'm caught between two worlds. In this world, life seems predictable and we are looking forward to dinners with friends, satisfying work and travel. In that other world, life seems uncertain and loss is inevitable.

"He's my dad. I need to be there. When I am there, I long to be here with you. But, when I am here, I want to be there with my dad." I start to cry. "What was it like for you when your dad died? Was it clear what to do?"

He puts his arms around me, and I feel his body soften. "No, it's never clear. You saw how I was when my dad died." He pauses. "I am going to miss you. Don't be away long."

I arrive at the airport the next morning with mixed emotions. Before I get on board, I call home for messages. My mom's voice is on the machine. "Dear, your dad is much better this morning. He is resting peacefully, and color has come back into his face. Call when you get in."

My stomach sinks. I feel tampered with, used, manipulated, like I have been unzipped once again.

Maybe I don't have to go back. Or maybe Mom is okay now. Or maybe she is only okay because she knows I am coming back. I had always been certain that if I just packed up my things and moved back home, into my little rosebud-wallpapered bedroom, that Mom and Dad would be fine.

I thought about Miriam, my cousin. Miriam was forty and still lived with her parents in New York. "I don't know what is wrong with that girl — no job, no career, no husband," my mother used to say to Aunt Clara.

"She looks just like a carbon copy of her mother. Did you see that bleached-blonde beehive hairdo and the long red nails?" Aunt Clara responded.

"She needs to lose some weight and get rid of that terrible Brooklyn accent, if she wants to find a good husband," I overheard Mom say. "It might be too late."

In my worst moments, I imagined that I could have been Miriam, but I escaped.

My ex-husband, the only Jew at Dartmouth and I found him. How resourceful of me! I was grateful. Confusing our long hidden escape fantasies with love, we poured out our hearts to one another. He was my ticket out of all I had endured. We rode the wave of exhilaration through senior year and married right after graduation. Away from the structure of school and the envy of our friends, we grew cranky and tired of each other as we drove farther and farther West to a pin point on the Rand McNally United States Road map — a tiny Indian Reservation in La Push, at the Northwest Corner of Washington State. On our first anniversary he gave me an umbrella. I began to see that his once-appealing practicality, intellect and retiring ways became confining — he was just another jailer. One year later we were divorced. I felt relieved. What did I know about marriage? Mom said I would fall in love and live happily ever after, but I didn't. I was too young and there was

Vietnam. He died in Da Nang a year later. His letters to me were still in his pocket. Years later, I felt a deep sense of loss. I never knew who he was.

During that time, Mom and Dad still told their friends and the neighbors that I was in graduate school in Heidelberg with their Dartmouth-educated, Jewish son-in-law. They didn't know that my husband had discovered Brian and me making love on the sofa in my girlfriend's apartment.

When I was sixteen, dreaming of Mr. Right, it wasn't those smart-alecky Jewish boys at my temple with their yarmulkes, big noses and oversized ears that caused me to sigh and roll over in bed while I explored my body to climax. It was my fantasy man out of "Gunsmoke" who looked exactly like Brian — tall, silent and easy to project just about everything on to.

Brian, in his black leather jacket, and blonde hair tossed down over his blue eyes, drove me crazy the day he rode up in his Velosette 500 motorcycle. He had traveled through Europe and Africa, and he could fix anything, large or small. He took my heart and all my other organs as well.

I stopped calling and writing to Mom and Dad after they threw a conniption fit about my living 'in sin with a Goy' in Berkeley. From then on, I didn't hear from them, and it was fine with me.

The summer of 1969, I took a graduate Abnormal Psychology class at the University of California, in a low-lying bungalow near Sather Gate. While the professor droned on about the early signs of psychosis in adults, the door caught a soft afternoon breeze and slowly swung open. My eyes lit on my mother and father standing in the hall outside, just before the door slammed shut. For the rest of the hour I wondered if they were really there, three thousand miles away from home or was their absence working havoc on my unconscious mind? Maybe I should be the patient and not the student.

At the end of class, it actually was a relief to find them waiting for me in the hall. They said they were on their way to Hawaii for a vacation and wanted to talk some sense into me. I resisted like a cat caught in a bag. Dad got pushy. "Come and have lunch with us. You look too skinny. We'll treat you."

I knew that was the first step toward my softening. I said no.

"Let's see your house. Maybe we can meet Brian," Dad offered.

"Is he at least Jewish?" Mom inquired. Dad gave her a look.

I ignored her and began walking toward the parking lot.

"Is he black?" By now my mother had a thin, shrill sound in her voice.

"Let's walk her to her car," Dad said stoically.

But instead of seeing my car, they saw my Honda 360cc motorcycle with upswept pipes and a low-rider seat. "You sold your car?" Shock registered on Dad's face.

"Oy gevalt!" My mother pressed her hand against her heart. "You'll give your father a heart attack yet!"

I drove away. Several months later Brian and I went into the Peace Corps. He convinced me that I needed a career change and a free trip as a bright-eyed Kennedy role model. I didn't give Mom and Dad my address in the Kalahari Desert of Botswana. As far as I was concerned, I no longer had a family.

My romance with Brian languished in the hundred and twenty degree temperatures. His job was to dig for water, but I don't think I ever saw him do anything except suck hard Christmas candy, read the works of Arthur Clarke and Robert Heinlein and complain for hours along with other volunteers about the delays in getting the proper equipment to do his job. Brian gave new meaning to the term "armchair supervisor."

The role I traded for elementary school teaching in Berkeley was starting a handicraft center in the middle of the desert. Claudia, a former Peace Corps volunteer, had set up a retail outlet, Botswanacraft, in the capital. I was to be the driving force behind the operations: mobilizing the natives, finding the teachers to make and identify some viable products to ship and sell in Europe and the States. It was easier said than done.

The heat of the day slowed down even the most prolific worker. Supplies were interminably slow to arrive from South Africa. There was no electricity, and water was at a premium. The thatched hut we lived in during the day served as a factory during business hours. The goats often got loose and ate the straw off the hut, exposing us to heat and wind. The sun hovered in a blood-red ball all day long. Everything was mud-colored, with a cloudless, powder-blue sky overhead. The vastness and the extremes of heat and cold made me feel speechless and insignificant. The Kalahari seemed to own the people. Not like the cornfields of Nebraska, where farmers sit on their tractors like kings on thrones, taming the soil from one horizon to the other.

There were huge iguanas and spiders. One morning I found a pink spider the size of a rat inside my sneaker. It reared up and attacked me. When I told one of the teachers, work stopped. Everyone ran home and came back with tin cans of kerosene. We spent the day pouring the liquid down little holes, the size of pinpricks, around the hut and watching millions of baby spiders swarm out. Then we stomped them dead with our shoes.

It was 1970. Spacemen had landed on the moon, thousands of miles away, boys I dated in college were fighting for their lives in a hell of mud, rain and dense brush. All this was going on while I was caught up in the zeitgeist of our decade wandering around a desert in Birkenstock sandals, wilting under the Kalahari glare, masquerading as the ideal Peace Corps volunteer. I was in search of dried cow dung — wet grassy texture wouldn't do. The older it was, before it decomposed, the better as fuel for our makeshift kiln.

I had blown in like tumbleweed from the psychedelic waste-land of Berkeley, California, dead-ended from experiments with psychedelic drugs, psychotropic plants, the emptiness of an unsatisfying career my mother had chosen for me. I wanted to get as far away as possible from my parents' disappointment in me. The only things I had left were energy and hope, and I wove them into a risk and the desire to reinvent myself at twenty-eight, based on Brian's pipe dreams. He had romanti-cized Africa: easy living, no need for money, warmth, freedom and creativity.

At first, the volunteers — Jeff and Fannie, Charlie and Ray, teachers at the school, Brian and I — sat in a banyan tree outside town most of the day. In the crook of its widest limb, we saw fields of wild poppies, an anomaly, stretch-ing outward into the heat rising off the desert. We grew high on dope. One day we realized that it may have been no mistake that David Livingston spent eight years in this village. Maybe he had found this ancient tree also. As the sun reached its zenith, he was as high as a kite, the way we were. The weed took my mind off my problems, which I kept to myself.

I was preoccupied and worried that I was pregnant. I took a trip to the hospital compound at the far end of the village. There the missionary doctor, Mr. Bolton, examined me and gave me a blood test. "I've heard about you!" he scolded. "What you think you are doing living with a man and not expecting to be pregnant?" He was so certain that the blood test he gave me would come back positive that he gave me a delivery date. Apparently, I was two months along.

For the first several months, we planned our trip home — a free trip was guaranteed by the Peace Corps. If we played our cards right, we could take the long way home around the world!

After awhile, we all seemed to have had our fill of each other and the free weed, as each of us drifted off to our projects. Except for Brian, of course. He was never free of weed.

My test results never came back. Dr. Bolton said that the vial had broken on the way to the capital city. He encouraged me to come back and take another test. By this time I lacked the energy to get out of bed. I didn't tell Brian about my problem. In such small quarters, I wanted to keep this to myself, just in case it was a false alarm.

Bushmen appeared one morning at our door accompanied by Mama Kosi Din Ba, the self-appointed leader of the handicraft center. They looked more Asian than African, were shorter than I, perhaps not even five feet tall, and they had honey gold skin and round faces, with high, wide cheekbones and Mongoloid eyelids.

The handsome younger man could have been a Burmese prince, except that he was wearing nothing but a loincloth. He carried a bow and arrows. They acted as if nothing much worthwhile had been invented since the Stone Age.

The older man wore a pair of patched-together safari shorts that had probably belonged to a visiting hunter a long time ago. The skin around his waist was deeply wrinkled and hung in folds, apparently from alternate periods of feast and famine.

The smiling men greeted Brian and me formally, and we exchanged pleasantries, even though neither side could understand the other. Then we shook hands. We gave them food and water.

They seemed profoundly dignified, graceful, self-confident and independent. It was fascinating to hear them talk: their language was full of clicks. I picked out five separate clicks.

Mama Kosi Din Ba demonstrated these, to my delight. One of the clicks sounded like the "tsk-tsk," you might make when you shake your head and scold a naughty child. Another click, which comes from a little farther back in the mouth, is like the sound that you would use to encourage your horse to move a little faster. The rest of the clicks sounded deeper and came from still farther back in the throat. At night the women sang these sounds around home fires or while walking down the dirt roads, in quivery tunes, like birds gone crazy in the full moon.

I heard them singing from under my mosquito netting at night and wondered how I had gotten myself into this predicament. Brian was snoring and clicking away, American-style, next to me.

Before they left, one of the Bushmen came over to me and put his hand about an inch away from my belly and smiled. Then he said something in clicks and sounds to Mama Kosi Din Ba. She smiled but said nothing.

Later that afternoon, she sat with me under the jacaranda tree outside the handicraft center. We looked out over the desert where game trails made scribbles through the dry and empty landscape. Mama said, "You seem very lonely here, America-girl. You miss your family. I have some thing for you." In her pocket she pulled out two tiger kittens. Each scrambled for safety under her skirt. "One is for your right hand, the other is for your left. Malowe and Malemo: left and right in Setswana."

"What did the Bushmen say to you?" I asked her as I petted the kittens.

"They told me about a woman you should see who could help you."

I shrank back. They knew?

"She lives in a little clearing not far from here. I will take you tomorrow."

I felt a profound fear and sadness. I had been found out by people I didn't know or understand, while my white friends didn't have a clue. I was desperate, but also grateful that Mama had plucked me out of myself with the aid of the Bushmen, and was going to help me. I had no clear view of safety. Where was the easy land of drive-in movies, shopping for new clothes with Mom, and Kennedy's volunteers, the country where I thought I knew all the rules? Where was the place I could go home to?

At dusk we walked out into the open desert, the red clay earth warm from the day, and turned off a worn trail into some brush that changed into a lush oasis. There, hidden from sight, was a hut with a corrugated metal roof. Inside the dimly lit room sat an old, gaunt lady with a colorful cloth wrapped around her head. She greeted me with extended hands. Mama spoke to her in a series of clicks and consonants until they came to some agreement. Then we drank some tea. I relaxed and became very sleepy. She offered me her bed to lie in. Mama sat by my side.

I awoke to the sound of a rooster, but it was still dark out. Mama said from nearby, "You had a baby spirit inside you, now you are free of it. You must rest before we leave." I felt groggy and my back ached from sleeping on a hard bed.

Later, as the sun came up over the horizon, she wrapped me in a blanket over my clothes and we made our way back to the handicraft center. All my organs hurt deep inside, and felt strange, as I made my way back home. I expected Brian to be angry that I hadn't been home, but Mama had told him that I was staying overnight with her family on their hunting land. He greeted me with a hug.

The several weeks that followed were a blur. I remained in my cot in the loft, upstairs from the factory. I could hear sounds below as Mama Kosi Din Ba provided the discipline in Setswana and set the tone of the place. She continued to teach everyone to perfect their pottery the traditional Botswana way. Much of their art had been desecrated by British and then

German missionaries. I heard them baking the clay pots in the pit, shoveling in the dried cow dung and covering the pit with corrugated tin.

I could smell the musty odor of the slow burning kiln and felt sad and self-critical because I wasn't doing my share.

While I was recuperating, Mama brought Ta Tooma to live with us because she had worked for the last white couple in the village, and she was to earn a small stipend by carrying water up from the river bed, cleaning and lighting the kerosene lamps, splitting wood, building a fire outside for cooking under the three-legged pot, throwing buckets of ash down the hole in the three-sided, walled outhouse, and, as a distraction between heavier jobs, pausing to kill snakes, spiders and iguanas.

Ta Tooma was a huge, strapping woman with athletic arms and legs. Her shoes alone, big rubber boots with untied laces, dwarfed ours when they sat outside the hut while she swept. She had two half-blind eyes. I didn't know which one to focus on. They looked like broken egg yolks, mixed slightly — big black eyes that were hard to reach into — a silent intruder in our lives. I was unused to servants, and felt incredibly guilty watching her work.

She spoke no English, so Mama, a little jet-black woman, gave her direction, often flailing her arms around with passion, elbows stuck out like wings.

One day a package arrived from Mom and Dad. The parcel, wrapped in a Saks Fifth Avenue shopping bag, contained my favorite type of cotton turtlenecks and hard candy. The package contained no messages, just the peace offerings and a return address.

As I slowly regained my health, I began staying away from Brian. There were days of long silences between us. I began to wonder why other volunteers remained in such a desolate and lonely place. And I couldn't understand how this new career would help me when I got back home. It seemed clear that Fannie was there because Jeff was avoiding the draft, as were the other guys. How about Susan Campton, a single volunteer living in Maun, in the Okavango Swamps up north?

I decided to go to visit her and find out for myself. Also I thought that maybe not having seen much of the country, we were given a particularly barren and primitive section of Botswana. Maybe others had it better. I took a train up through Buyawayo to Maun. Through the window, I saw that all of Botswana, as far as the eye could see, was dry, uninhabitable desert. Game trails made scribbles on dry earth in the barren desert.

In the Kalahari it seemed like a full-time job just keeping a step ahead of the environment. A casual tourist wouldn't last long in the Kalahari. In all its 100,000 square miles there is no reliable source of water.

When I arrived, the sky grew dark. A brown cloud filled the air. Everyone ran for cover. I ran into the only store I could find as a clicking and flapping sound grew louder and louder. Suddenly, the sound was ear-splitting. Gigantic shiny black locusts slammed themselves into the windows and thatch of the store. Children shrieked. I stood there paralyzed until the bombardment subsided.

The Maun locals ran out of the store and began gathering dried grass and weed, grabbing anything that would burn. Others gathered the dead locusts, and over open fires they baked and ate the insects.

With gestures, a small boy and his friends led me to Susan's hut. I shouted her name long before I got to her thatched door. It stood ajar. Inside lay Susan on her cot reading *Gone with the Wind: The Classic Comic Book Edition.*

We spent two days together, sharing food and talking. Then I got to the purpose of my visit. Why was she in this God-forsaken place?

"You know, I was born and raised in Manhattan, Kansas," Susan said. "No one in my family ever left Kansas — four generations of farmers. I have done something with my life. I went somewhere. The first of every month, I send each one of my five brothers a postcard from the Okavango Swamps in the Kalahari Desert. Do you know what a thrill that gives me?"

My heart sank. I thought she was here on some noble cause. She could give me a higher meaning and purpose.

On the train back, I met Maureen and Joshua, Baha'i missionaries living on the far side of my village. By the end of the trip, I had persuaded Maureen to take me on one of her conversions. I was certain that Maureen might be inspired, and through her I could find a purpose in being here.

"We are enormously successful in converting these Africans to Baha'i. Last year we made 100% of our goal." When I got off the train, I had a copy of the Baha'i literature in my backpack, and a promise to go with Maureen a few days later on her next trip to a local village. We were going to convert a whole tribe of Thamaga.

Maureen's Volvo sprayed up dust and sand. Desperate for connection, I felt like a refugee from a prisoner-of-war camp. I hadn't sat in a luxury car for a year and a half.

The conversion amounted to nothing more than Maureen throwing pamphlets, like the one she gave me, into open doors of huts, because she was afraid to get out of her car. When she dropped me off at her pink stucco house after a dusty day, I begged off dinner.

Meanwhile, the packages from Mom kept coming. With them came short letters. I wrote back, trying to communicate the daily life of the village, somewhat unsuccessfully, and staying away from any heated topics.

Dear Mom,

A strange mongrel began hanging around our center. We discovered through Mama that this dog belonged to two Baha'i missionaries who lived in the only European-type house near the center of the town. He is friends with Malemo, my tiger cat. Malowe, my other cat, ran off or was eaten one night while we slept. I was very sad about this.

Their bush dog began coming around and sitting inside our hut on the dirt floor, watching our cat. Mama Kosa Din Ba named them (That's what we call her — everyone is Mama here) when she brought them to me as kittens because she thought I was homesick.

The kitten took a liking to Sock, short for Socrates the dog, and the Baha'i missionaries began coming around to drag their dog home.

Brian joked that the dog only liked white people, why else would he choose to hang out with us? The Motswanas chased the dog, because he had part sheep dog in him, and he would veer off from our walk together and herd the half-starving sheep. This made the sheep owners irate. They would run after Sock and try to beat him with their staffs.

I met this Jewish intern from the mission hospital. He is here for some health organization. He led us on a trip into an old deserted missionary house near a dried river bed. White butterflies flew up in our faces. The house was still intact even though it was abandoned more than one hundred years ago. Can you imagine?

Thank you for the candy and turtlenecks. I really miss you and love you. Thanks for finding me again.

Your loving daughter

Several weeks later, I received a letter from my mother.

> *My Dear,*
> *We love you very much. If there is anything we*
> *can do to help, please let us know. Your dad and I just*
> *want you to be happy. You are our only daughter. We*
> *don't want to lose our connection to you. Our love to*
> *Brian, and thank Mama for looking after you.*
> *Love, Mom and Dad*

I cried, a deep outpouring of many months, for not being able to tell my mother about the pregnancy, and for her loving me despite all the pain I had caused her. Brian thought it had something to do with him. Suddenly, he started to make things better for us. He bought a 90cc Honda motorcycle from a departing volunteer, installed an empty drum for a rainwater tank for showers (cold because we didn't have hot water) and an outdoor toilet with a real white American toilet seat on it.

Then something very strange happened. A German guy drove up to our hut looking for the road to the capital city. In his truck, he had machine guns lining the inside of his van. He introduced himself as an ex-pat from Germany. He had been roaming around the desert since 1943. The next morning something clicked in my mind. A spring unloaded, and I couldn't get out of that place fast enough. I had to leave. The German gun-runner was just one more strange experience, but he was the straw the broke this camel's back.

I packed my knapsack and left everything else behind. I said goodbye to Brian. I felt sad leaving him, after we'd gone through so much together. We eased the pain by making torrid love on the dirt floor of the hut one last time. I got the feeling that Brian wasn't going to get much good sex for awhile. Then

I did my leave-taking of Jeff, Fannie and Mama and walked halfway to the capital city.

When I got tired, I sat under the tree, like all the other locals waiting for the next empty truck headed to the center of town. I walked right up to the door of the Peace Corps director and told him I quit. He didn't put up a fight.

I collapsed on the plane and ended up in a London hospital for a month, diagnosed with acute hepatitis. I hadn't been pregnant, after all. I felt cynical and disillusioned with Dr. Bolton, Mama, and everyone for awhile. That marked the moment when I grew up. Mom and Dad flew to London and stayed there while I convalesced, but I was no longer my mother's child. I had softened toward her. I could finally face her as I was, not who she wanted me to be. I no longer was ashamed of myself, because I had taken hold of my life by leaving. I was going to find my own purpose, and not tag after a man.

8

I didn't have a clue that a contract was out on my life.

When I got back from Botswana, I called my old therapist, Jan Rie. She was a good woman, but she knew that she had a basket case on her hands. Then, out of the blue, Carol Barts appeared at Jan's house. Carol was a freshly divorced, attractive and athletic-looking blonde. She had four kids ranging from seven to sixteen, and was on a mission of her own. Carol had recently blown in from Montana, with a pile of money and a dream in her heart. She was positive as the day was long, a real cheerleader among women.

She immediately bought a mansion on the edge of the Pacific Ocean in Aptos. "I got it for a song," she said in her lilting Midwestern voice, when I first met her. I was sure she had been the most popular girl at Helena High School.

Jan had a knack for matchmaking, because the deal was, I was to stay at Carol's for the summer while I got myself back on my feet, in exchange for fixing up her house, and looking after Dan, the seven-year-old, and being big sister to Charlene and Kate.

I didn't see the mansion until moving day. Upon my entrance through the gates, a circular driveway ushered me to the front door. I saw a crack in the cement, and it widened as I walked into the foyer and stood in the center of the living room. At its widest, the crack was about two inches. I followed it out to the Olympic-size pool, across the patio, past the hot tub and the gardens until finally it ended at the gigantic Plexiglas windscreen at the edge of the cliff. In front of me was the cerulean blue of the vast Pacific Ocean.

Beneath my feet, I imagined the tectonic plates of the San Andreas Fault moving and shifting. This was the song Carol was talking about.

But look, if it didn't bother her, why should it bother me? We had bigger problems to deal with than an earthquake in the first chapter of the 'seventies in California.

For example, I was going through dire culture shock. California had changed from two years earlier. Before I left, people were hiding pot inside the tops of their toilet bowls and when I returned, I saw drivers smoking it on the freeway. Carol was going through a traumatic divorce, and her kids were out of their minds trying to adjust to the California lifestyle.

Jan made me promise one thing. I had to attend a growth group of hers each Saturday at her home in Pescadero. That's where I met Halston Kirk Waller.

Carol and I went together. I was the youngest one in the group. Most of the women were divorced or on the verge. And then there was Halston, known as Kirk, a black man with a Dashiki, huge pepper-and-salt Afro and an angular face, with a plastic pocket protector inserted in his white button-down shirt. He rarely spoke for the duration of the workshop.

We sat on overstuffed pillows in a room that was empty, except for the wall-to-wall carpet, and tried to learn how to become art therapists.

I was grappling with the demons of another failed phase of my life, but immediately I felt chemistry with Kirk. "You are multi-faceted and very complex," he whispered to me, during the break, after I had poured my heart out during a visualization exercise preceding a clay sculpture I made and presented to the group.

He smelled of some indefinable scent, something from my childhood that I later discovered was Canoe. It should have been outlawed, along with drugs.

I hadn't known this kind of kindness, much less this new term, "feedback." Jan gave us several rules, but it seemed like Kirk was an old hand at this process, and indeed he was.

"I'm a theologian," he said. He worked as a full professor at the Theological Seminary in San Francisco, and had written a book called *Sex and Spirit*. I had never met an author before, and I was impressed that someone could have the discipline to sit down and write what was in his heart and mind.

So on a calm sunny day in the middle of August, Kirk and I tried to integrate our sexuality and spirits in the warm heather on the slopes of Mt. Tamalpais. I was Natalie Wood to his Warren Beatty in our own special version of *Splendor in the Grass*. Students were integrating in Arkansas, lunch counters were integrating across Alabama, and I was doing my own personal integration — so fashionable in the early 'seventies in Berkeley and across the country.

As the summer waned, Charlene, Kate, and Dan were making plans to head back to school while Don, Carol's eldest son, was going on to college. Carol was starting school at the University of Santa Cruz in their doctoral program. I felt like a fifth wheel. My life was adrift, and the culture shock hadn't lessened. I felt closer to black people, after spending time with so many in such close quarters in Botswana.

So I decided to move up to Berkeley to be closer to Kirk.

Somehow it didn't matter that he was married with a small child and one more on the way.

I moved back into the old house that Brian and I owned with several other people near the campus. Up in the large attic room that spanned the footprint of the house, I set up shop. I put down two California king-size mattresses with large pillows. This was where Brian and I used to sleep. Then I set up a kind of studio apartment for myself, so that I wouldn't have to spend time downstairs with the three other tenants.

I found a job filling in for an art teacher who was on maternity leave at the local high school. The janitor, Charlie, another black guy with a huge Afro, convinced the principal that I could use the stage in the auditorium for an art room, because of the cramped quarters in the building.

One day, Kirk picked me up at school, and Charlie really looked him over. After that Charlie seemed even friendlier toward me. Kirk came and went from my house. My roommates didn't say anything; we knew better than to bum each others' trip. Live and let live was our philosophy.

I wanted to know everything I could about Kirk — where he did his work, how he could write, I poured out my heart to him one day in front of Sproul Plaza. I wanted to be just like him. "I can't seem to make anything work in my life," I cried. "Here I am, thirty-one, and I have no real career. You are thirty-five and everything works for you."

"I started early," he joked. His "mammy" in Tennessee taught him to believe that the few strands of straight hair on his head were "good hair." "If time and money were no object, what would you really love to do?" he asked.

"I want to get a doctor's degree, like you. I've wanted to go back to school and study psychology for so many years."

In that moment, he leaned down and took my hands, looked me straight in the eyes and gave me back to myself.

"That is what you are going to do," he said. "You gotta make a commitment to your own growth and development, and not just wait until the next guy comes along."

So I did. I made out applications to thirteen doctoral programs, just in case twelve rejected me.

Kirk had mixed feelings. He wanted me to stay. Whenever he wasn't home, he was at my house, except during the prime time of families: Friday, Saturday night and all day Sunday. When he was with me, we made love on my California king bed.

He used words like "bootie," "twang," "the naughty," and "take it on home, sister." He said dirty things in my ears, things Jewish boys just didn't know. He said, "I want to marry you."

"But you are married," I answered incredulously.

"I want you to live with Patrice and me and little Raymond and our new baby. I want you to be part of our family. When I married Patrice, I loved her, and now I love you. And I want you to be part of our family."

I felt flattered, yet thought he was crazy. I didn't say anything. Why tamper with a good thing?

Around midnight one night, at the height of our lovemaking, my roommate knocked loudly at my bedroom door. He was a cool guy named Chick.

"There's someone who wants to see you down at the front door. She asked if Kirk was here."

I was on automatic, as I followed Chick downstairs. He went back to his room, and I opened the door. In the light of the front porch, I saw a very lean, attractive black woman.

"I'm here to get Kirk," she said. Her black eyes burned holes into my face. I could feel her rage. I knew I couldn't bullshit her.

"He's sleeping," I said.

"If he doesn't get his ass home in fifteen minutes, he's going to find all his shit on the street," she said as she turned on her heels and left. I went upstairs and woke Kirk.

"I think your wife wants you home, right now," I said.

"What?" He looked at me sleepily and smiled as he reached for me.

"I'm not kidding. She was just at the front door and said that if you don't come home now, she's going to throw all your stuff out on the street."

I thought Kirk was his own man, but I never saw a man jump up so fast, throw on his clothes and get out of there. I didn't hear from him for several days. I felt depressed and rejected. He finally called me on the third day.

"I explained everything to Patrice, and she is okay with it." I was incredulous.

"She wants you to come over tonight for a party we are having at our home. Come about seven and the three of us can talk," he said.

I spent the whole day finding and discarding clothes to wear that night. I finally chose an emerald mini-skirt, tight black sleeveless top and spiked heels. Something that showed off my thin legs and arms.

I drove over to his side of town, which by the way, was becoming the right side of Berkeley. I happened to live on the wrong side. He lived on a cul-de-sac of tree-lined streets right near the university.

I parked my car and walked into his stucco home in the white middle-class neighborhood. His wife greeted me as if nothing had ever happened. As she fed her son, Kirk took me downstairs to see his office where he wrote his famous book, *Sex and Spirit*. I was surprised and shocked to see that it was a windowless room with a child's desk next to the boiler. This was his office. On the wall across from his desk was a life-size photo of his nude wife. I felt betrayed, but I hid my reaction. Here I had thought that his book was written in a spacious and glamorous setting, not behind a boiler somewhere.

Upstairs, the music was starting, and Patrice introduced me to waves of black people who were her friends. One told me that Patrice was four months pregnant.

I wondered who they must think I was, since I was the only white woman there. Later I discovered what she had up her sleeve.

We danced until three in the morning. First it was Kirk and Patrice, then it was Kirk and me. Then we danced in groups to the throbbing music of Sly and the Family Stone, Roberta Flack and Donny Hathaway, and John Lee Hooker. I felt oddly like I was part of a family and that I was being watched at the same time.

At school the following Monday, Charlie took me aside in the lunchroom. "I don't know what you think you are doing," he said, "but some dudes came by this morning and asked me about you. What you up to anyway?"

I looked at him, dumbfounded. He saw that I didn't have a clue.

"Just be careful of your back," he said.

"Why are you trying to scare me?" I asked.

"Because you are playing with fire."

Kirk called several days after the party. By that time, I was beginning to feel weird about being in his house with his kid and his pregnant wife. I didn't have him during prime time and she was going to have another one of his kids. I was bound to lose, and I knew that. He didn't have any plans on leaving her, from what he told me. He had this idea that I'd just be added to the family, like a white nanny or something.

I called her the next evening. "Thank you for inviting me to your party. I really enjoyed myself. I called because I wondered if we could talk privately."

The next evening, she rang my doorbell about seven. Chick answered the door and freaked. "Whoa," he said, "the dude you are looking for isn't here tonight."

She laughed. "No, I'm here for a meeting. It's cool."

I took her upstairs and we sat down on the bed. That was really the only place to sit, even though it was awkward. "I have to tell you that I am really sorry about getting involved with Kirk. Maybe it was your opening your home and buying that bunch of crap from Kirk about me becoming part of the family. No offense, but I don't want to become part of your family. When I saw your home and your family, I felt bad about what I had done. Can you forgive me? I'm just hurting."

That's when I told her about returning from Botswana adrift, meeting Kirk at the growth group, the Canoe fragrance and the rest.

At first, she was wary of me. But then she cried and I cried. She didn't say much, but she seemed like she was listening. Finally she said, "I don't think you are aware of this, but there is a contract out in the black community for you. That's what we do when a white woman comes along and messes with our men."

I was stunned. "You didn't have to tell me. Thank you."

I don't think I ever heard from Kirk after that party and the meeting with Patrice. He seemed to fade into the background like so much figure and ground of the gestalt of that time. But it didn't matter, because several days later, I got my acceptance letter to the University of Massachusetts graduate program and my attention started turning away. I was packing and getting ready to drive across country to the next chapter in my life. Botswana and its aftermath were behind me.

When I asked Charlie about the contract, he pretended to be stunned, and then he copped to knowing about it. "I told you to stay away from him, you were playing with fire. I helped you out and you didn't even know it." I wondered if he was telling the truth or whether it was more black bullshit to scare a little white Jewish girl.

Later on, when I called Carol and told her that I too, was in a doctoral program, I felt a stiff cool breeze blow between us, as if somehow I had invaded her territory. So I confided in her about the last chapters of my romance with Kirk. She told me that he had had affairs with every one of the women in the Gestalt Art Therapy Group before I had gotten there. They just were amused to watch him work his magic on me.

"You mean, he asked the others to be a part of his family also?"

"And more," she laughed. I felt had. Several years later, after many females failed to be recruited to his family tribe, Patrice left him with her two kids and moved to Guyana with Jim Jones.

9

My father is resting comfortably when I arrive at the hospital. I look at him while he sleeps. In my mind I go over my personal checklist to reassure myself: How does he look? Is his skin gray or pinker? Is he perky or listless? Is he interested in people around him, or quiet and uncommunicative? Are there more or fewer tubes in him? Maybe he will recover and be around when my book comes out. I want him to be there to enjoy that with me.

On the other hand, he seems thinner, but he is breathing more on his own. The doctor said that if he could breathe on his own, he could leave the hospital. After all, even a nursing home would be better than this.

Is he is dying inch by inch, or he is reclaiming his life inch by inch? It is beginning to seem like a tie. I sit in the chair by the side of the bed and hold his hand as he dozes.

He wakes and begins rasping aloud. His rasps became intelligible sounds. "I could have been somebody." His mouth is forming words. "I had so many opportunities. I could have been like Benny Goodman or Glenn Miller. Why didn't I use those opportunities? Instead, I squandered them."

Shopping Lessons

My dad says that he was a famous musician for a time before the Depression. He led The Saul Perlman Band in Newark, New Jersey, in "The Battle of the Bands" on radio. Dad played against Benny Goodman and Glenn Miller, and won the radio competitions.

Tears appear and stream silently down his stoic face. At first they are imperceptible, but then the wet shines like glass, so it registers with me as unmistakable grief. I have never seen him cry before.

My mind is objective and analytical. I am thinking that this is a hard way to cry, not like my tears, with the loud sobbing, pinched face and flushed wet skin. What I see are his opaque brown eyes softening, then pleading, wanting to attach themselves to me. But I feel nothing but curiosity, and I am thinking that I can't understand why I am feeling nothing.

My dad, values the mind while each part of his system is shutting down.

He has been babbling, sometimes on and off, for days. My mother is disgusted with him.

"You must fight this, Saul. *Kaynahorah* (ward off evil). You cannot die. Saul, Saul!" Her voice is low and scolding. "You are imagining. Please wake up."

I sit by his bedside and try to make sense of what he is saying. Maybe he is trying to send an important message to me. Now he is speaking clearly enough. He is telling me that he is going to see a man in New York, alone and at night. The man has a secret invention that will make him rich.

"Tell me, what it is, Dad? What's the invention? What is it?"

He smiles softly, "Oh, I can't tell. Not even you, my love." His small brown eyes dart left and right and back again, but he doesn't see me. He is in his own world.

My mother sits in the corner, scowling. "It's the medication," she says sourly. She is infused with grief and fear.

I lean over him, waiting for the pictures to flood in. Silent. Then I imagine the sounds of him practicing his violin in the living room. The squawk that came out of that thing, and how it awakened something in my mother's body and voice, something sexual and young. It was one of the few times I saw her giggle and dance around the living room, past the velvet sofas with their plastic covers and lamps with expensive silk shades. Her flaccid body undulating, she lifted up her skirt with both hands and veered toward my dad. Now with a love of my own, I understand their strange love signals, but back then, when I witnessed this, I turned away. She had suddenly become a stranger.

He met Mom one moonlit night up at Kiamesha Lake, where he was playing at a club. They fell in love, despite her mother's warning that it was the Depression and they should be careful, should wait. She became pregnant with Harry, and Dad had to get a real job.

Now, in the hospital, his eyes are moist with tears, and he begins to cry. "I could have been somebody. I had an opportunity and I let it go. I could have been a Glenn Miller or a Benny Goodman," he repeats.

I lean over and take his hand, and let those eyes find a home in me. "Dad, maybe that wasn't your destiny. Maybe your destiny was to raise two kids: Harry and me. We are your music. We are your legacy."

He smiles, closes his eyes, and dozes off peacefully. I have reassured him, but I have my own doubts.

It is the second week of April, just before Easter. We haven't turned the clocks forward yet. The air has a bite to it, left over from winter. Mud covers the parking lot outside.

The ICU is quiet. Dr. Arnstein stands at the door. "Your dad probably won't make it through the next twenty-four hours," he states, then turns and leaves.

Tonight Mom has promised Dr. Arnstein that she won't have him revived if there is another crisis, but the line of how much we can take keeps shifting.

Dad is moving in and out of a coma. At times he seems to be listening, and at other times his eyes are vacant.

When my mother is out of the room, I whisper to him, "Dad, it's time to go. I love you."

I feel like a burglar, intruding into a carefully guarded space. But I can't take it any longer. No one ever talked to him about his own dying. We always act like he will get better, even now.

The room smells of deteriorating flesh, like towels that are burning in the hot sun. When I move close to Dad, I gag from the odor.

Mom returns. "I called Harry. He will be here soon," she reports, without emotion. We sit motionless and waiting.

Dad shows no signs of recognition when Harry, Roberta and Francine arrive. I feel overwhelmed with anxiety when I see Harry again. There seem to be so many things to cope with at one time. We stand around at the far side of the room, whispering and making small talk. Roberta puts a flower next to Dad's head, one that she has taken from a vase at the nurse's station. She is weeping softly. Mom disapprovingly whips the flower off the bed and angrily hands it back to her.

"He doesn't want that! He's not dead yet!" she whispers angrily. "What is wrong with that woman?" she turns to me and says under her breath.

They leave shortly after that, saying that Harry still has a long drive and has to go to work the next morning.

At ten o'clock, Mom and I walk across the dimly-lit parking lot of the hospital and drive home in a soft spring drizzle, the kind where you can't decide whether to turn on the wipers. I am thinking about this when Mom turns to me and asks, "What should I do? Should I have Dad taken off the respirator?"

For months I have harbored silent resentment toward my mother for keeping Dad alive because she can't let him go, but each time she actually asks me this question, I find that I answer with my heart.

"Mom, if it were my husband, I don't know what I would do."

Mom and I are preparing for bed. I still smell that burning towel odor around me as I try to drop off to sleep. I wonder how that odor could have gotten in my clothes when I didn't touch Dad.

I hear the telephone ring in my parents' room. Then the night-light in the hallway creates a dark outline of my mom as she stands in my bedroom doorway. "It's the hospital. Dad is going. Put on your clothes. He may be gone by the time we get there."

I jump out of bed, throw on my clothes and meet Mom downstairs. We rush out of the house into the damp April night. The silent streets glisten as I drive the Buick Regal through Maplewood to South Orange into Livingston.

After all these months, I can't believe it will soon be over. I can't imagine how that will feel. I see a little old woman beside me. Everything about her seems frail. I notice her hands resting on her lap, so much smaller than my own small hands.

The nurse stands by his bedside. She points to the monitor on the left of the respirator. It is a little black and white television set, with a line bouncing across the middle of the screen. The bouncing line is getting straighter and straighter.

"See this line?" the nurse asks. "When it goes flat he is gone."

For eight months, that line that has been fluctuating steadily in the middle of the screen. It is one indicator of the breadth and depth of my dad's life. It comes down to one line.

The respirator continues to breathe for him, that in-and-out wind sound that fills the room, but the heart monitor no longer registers anything. It is indeed a thin line on the screen. My dad is gone. And that is it.

The nurse leaves.

I know that my dad goes to his grave with his music still left inside him.

Mom speaks first. "What shall we say? Let's say the twenty-third psalm." We stand over his bed awkwardly.

"The Lord is my shepherd, I shall not fear," I begin.

"No, no, that isn't the way it goes. Let me get a book." She rushes out of the room.

I continue the psalm alone with my dad. Improvising. Wondering how nineteen years of Reform Judaism could leave me with so little.

Then I just sit with Dad in the stillness. I get up from the chair and walk over to the side of the bed. I lean over his body. I stare at him for quite a while. Then I put my hand on his chest. It feels hard, bony and filled with fluid. I open his eyes and see a cloudy confused look there. I hear my dad's quiet voice say to me, "Take care of your mother."

I feel a little push from behind and know that I have moved up in the queue. At that moment a new chapter is beginning, of which I understand very little. My body feels numb and tired, but my mind is very clear and calm.

My mother returns with Rabbi Gruen. "Pray for him," she commands.

The rabbi is unmoved. "In Judaism, your rabbi doesn't do the praying over a dead man. You do it. Just say the *Shema*." Then he leaves.

Mom looks at me and shrugs. "I've got to call everybody. You stay here. I'll call the funeral home. Don't let anyone touch the body."

She grabs her purse, pulls out her address book and flies out of the room.

A while later, a woman comes in and washes down Dad's body. Mom stands in the corner of the room and watches. Neither Mom nor I can pick up a washcloth to do it. I could have created a sacred ritual of that out of my love for my father. I could have pulled down the covers and touched his body for the last time, seen how his skin had atrophied into blue and green tones, let the stench of his deterioration permeate my pores, noticed how his withered torso had withstood the eight months of pain lying in a hospital bed. But I didn't. I have never touched my dad's naked body in life, and in death it mortifies me.

Another, older nurse comes in. She takes out all the catheters that have supplied nourishment and evacuated waste those eight months. He lies hard and still now. No more fighting to stay alive to be with my mom.

Mom used to tell me stories about her nursing career when I was small, "You are born alone and you die alone. People slip away in the early morning hours mostly, because they don't want their relatives to be there." Loved ones have a way of hanging on.

And so it was with my dad.

From Dad's window, I see the night sky open to the dawn light over South Mountain Reservation. Two middle-aged men dressed in black double-breasted suits come into the hospital room and introduce themselves as morticians from Bernstein's funeral home. My mother directs the operation of moving my dad's body onto a gurney and wheeling it away.

We drive home at sunrise. I feel relieved that it is finally over, and exhausted from staying awake all night. Inches away, grief beyond understanding is hiding in the shadows.

10

I didn't know that my body could betray me so, but like Dad's, mine had also, several years earlier. "You have a lump no larger than the size of a pea," he proclaimed as he felt my right breast.

It all seemed like a bad dream. I had called Dr. Bear, a gynecologist, for an annual pap smear, and scheduled it for five o'clock on a Friday after a long work week.

I rolled into his office precisely on time efficient in my little blue suit and panty hose. A little errand — in and out — I thought. Then I could start my weekend.

The doctor had a thin face. His head seemed larger than his body. I reflected, *I should really find myself a woman gynecologist.* It had been a seed mulching in the back of my mind for several years.

"Here, feel it." He pressed my hand on top of my breast. A strange territory. My doctor knew this area better than I do.

At first, his words didn't register in my mind. "Do you do breast self- exams?" he asked.

"No." I looked up at him. Wrong answer. My face reflected in his glasses. His concern was starting to sink in.

"Get dressed. I'll give you the name of a surgeon," he said matter of factly. "You have a lump the size of a pea. Here, feel." Sure enough, there it was under the skin. I moved it around.

Panic kicked in. "Now, wait a minute! What is this? How many patients do you see a month?" He must have something up his sleeve, I thought suspiciously.

He blinked dispassionately as he looked at me.

"Oh, about two hundred."

"And how many do you find have lumps?"

"About one or two," he answered.

Now I felt sick with fear.

"Why a surgeon? Surgeons cut. What is he going to cut?" I heard myself thinking out loud.

"He will do a biopsy and see if it is malignant," he answered.

Malignant or benign. *Malignant is the bad word.*

I frantically grasped at control now.

"I want the names of women doctors. An older woman, someone who is older than me, not a man," I demanded. A woman would be more comforting. She would tell me this was not true.

I pictured men with their hands and fingers shaped like sides of beef grasping at my tiny breast, as if trying to find the opening of a needle to thread. I didn't want to feel victimized by an insensitive male.

He spoke very slowly and patiently. "They don't come that way. Women weren't let into medical school until the late nineteen-seventies. I could give you the name of a woman near your age, if you like."

I left with two names. I drove home in a state of shock and told David. He became frantic and made me make an appointment with one of them early Monday morning. He worried all weekend and it wasn't comforting me.

I couldn't believe this was happening to me.

I had always eaten right. I exercised. I wondered occasionally why my generation felt guilty about eating food. I ate low fat-foods, although I frequently joked that food was "face entertainment." My unhealthy thoughts had all been noted-anger at David for small transgressions, resentment against my mother's prying; covetous fantasy acts against my co-workers. Body and mind are connected, I had read. I was determined not to act impulsively and rush to surgery.

On the following Monday I appeared at the surgeon's office. A woman about ten years my junior greeted me. She had a brittle smile and a wiry, tall frame. Her dark hair was combed back into a tight knot. I noted her long, thin delicate fingers.

This was Adele Smyth. She looked like an aerobics teacher. She had been in practice eight months in an office of older male surgeons. The men had given her the smallest office, with a child's size desk. A magazine clipping on the wall near the reception area boasted of her performing surgery during an earthquake after being in practice for only eight weeks.

"I don't care if she can do surgery on one foot," my husband said. "She is not logging in flying time with you to get her wings." We crossed her off our list.

We found another woman surgeon. On the examining table, Dr. Victoria Verdun felt my breasts. "I will just take a needle aspiration," she said.

"Are you going to cut anything?"

"It will just take a second, and it won't hurt." Before I could protest, Dr. Verdun drew fluid from a long-nosed needle and pulled it sharply from my breast.

"We'll know if it's malignant by morning," she said. I felt betrayed.

The next evening when I came home from work, there was a message on my answering machine. "This is Dr.

Verdun, your biopsy shows a malignant tumor. Call me to schedule surgery immediately."

My life was getting away from me. I went into high anxiety.

The test showed that I was at risk of dying of breast cancer.

I always thought that others would leave me first and I'd be alone, but I never thought I would die. I would be leaving a party that was just getting into full swing, and missing all the excitement, or having to go to bed early in summer while it was still light out.

David began calling other surgeons and setting up interviews with them. He wanted to get information, to be comprehensive and make the right decision.

There was Dr. Sheelon, the artist type, whose picture of his mentor hung on the wall. Occasionally, he would talk directly to his mentor and then to us. Dr. Murray was two hours late for the appointment and Dr. Hansen acted like a brain and a spinal cord — no heart or humanity.

When we went back to Dr. Verdun, she was cold and brisk. When David asked her what she would do if it were her breasts, she responded, "I would cut off these jugs, don't need them anymore, I've suckled two children."

David and I looked at each other. The thought of slicing off a part of your body because it has served its purpose only confirmed her unsuitability. "Who knows what else she would deem to slice off you, while you were asleep on the operating table," David said to me, once we were back in our car.

We were at a loss.

My mother was calling every day with any information she could find. She was faxing us and sending us newspaper clippings and books. She was threatening to come out and get this resolved. Several months passed.

One night in late April, David and I went out to dinner and were walking back to the car. The cherry blossoms had fallen on the wet sidewalk from the rain, making it look like snow. It was so lovely that I commented on it.

He said quite abruptly, "I am going to miss you. I don't want you to die."

I was shocked. Up to that point, I had a fatalistic attitude toward life. If my time was up, it was up. But suddenly, I felt an energy rise in my belly all the way up to my heart. "Hell, no, I'm not planning to die, I'm not going to let another woman, a new wife of yours, drive my car and sleep in my bed with my husband. I'm going to live!"

He said with feigned shock, "You put your car before me?" I realized what I had just said and we laughed together. Something shifted with us.

Shortly after that, we found a doctor we felt we could trust, who created realistic expectations for my condition. Then I called my mother. "I'm going in for surgery tomorrow. Don't come out. David and I can handle it."

"What, you don't want your mother and father? Put us up at the Tiburon Lodge, I'll make chicken soup. Be sure to get a toaster for your dad. He likes toast in the morning."

"Mom, my husband is perfectly capable of helping me."

It was only much later that we realized that David and I had deepened our bond of marriage, and Mom and I broke one more tie of childhood.

11

The morning after my father's death, I find Mom standing at the sink, looking out the open kitchen window at the lilac bush. The subtle fragrance of lilacs drifts into the small room and mingles with the smell of coffee. Mom has already made whole-wheat raisin bagels for me, and set a coffee cup on the table.

"I used to cut those big, purple ones and bring them into the house for Dad's dinner table," she said, nodding towards the bush. "I planted those when we moved in here. Can forty years go like *makkes* (nothing)?" She gestures with her palms up and her fingers open.

No more trekking up South Orange Avenue to see Dad in his hospital bed smiling wanly from behind all the tubes and machines. I feel a strange mixture of sadness and relief.

Mom sighs and smiles. "Sleep well, my *Oytser* (treasure)?"

I nod.

I smile at her words. It was a term she used when she tucked me into bed as a child. I bite into the hard crust of the dry toasted bagel. It is just the two of us here. No Daddy, no Dad, no father, no Bernie. No one to distract Mom. I feel ashamed at the secret delight I feel now that I have Mom all to myself. I can have the intimacy I longed for all these years. Almost as if she reads my mind, she asks excitedly,

"Who will go on your book tours?"

"I'll go alone."

"Not with David?"

"No, he won't travel."

"Can I go with you?"

"And be my manager?" I joke.

"Yes, I am the mother and your manager," she laughs.

"We'll travel together. You'll move to California and live with David and me. I'll take good care of you. We'll shop!"

I can't stand the abyss we are looking into this morning. It is just like me, in my excitement, to offer something that, maybe, I can't make good on. But I want to find a way to give her something to look forward to. Can't we always figure out the details later? Sure, if I think a moment I know that David would go crazy at the idea, and living with Mom would be a mixed bag. I'm not even sure if that's what I want. But I do know that I want something from her.

"It's a deal!" she exclaims. "If my body holds out."

"Why not get a physical?" I ask.

"Because I'm sure Dr. Arnstein would kill me, too."

"I thought you liked him."

"I'm just *farmutchet* (weary) of him," she reveals. "I'm not sure Dad did that well by him."

This is the first time I realize that my mom dislikes Dr. Arnstein. She knows how to hide deep emotion within shallow conversation or a passing smile. It gives her an impenetrable cover. Tragically, I have come to accept this cover, and am always shocked to momentarily see beneath it. Momentarily.

"We have to get to Bernstein's before ten," she says, changing the subject. "I've got to bring Dad's suit, shirt and trousers to the undertaker."

"How about shoes?" I ask.

"They don't bury people in shoes. No shoes." She pauses, then goes on. "I actually wondered about that myself. Aunt Helen said it's a Jewish thing. Probably, so that he is lighter when he floats to heaven." She lets out a little-girl laugh. I am happy to see that Mom seems to be coping, at least for now.

Bernstein's is located on Millburn Avenue, near Saks. I have probably driven past there a million times, but I never noticed it before today. It is one of those big, old brown-shingled mansions. Mom sits quietly until I pull into the driveway of the mortuary. "Park in the back, Dear. Mr. Rubin told me that we could go through the back entrance," she says.

I get out of the car and open the trunk to get the box of Dad's clothes. Mom runs ahead, scurrying in her little white sneakers. I carry the box into a thickly carpeted, large, open room.

Mr. Rubin is one of the men in black suits from the hospital the day before. "I'm sorry," he offers to both of us, averting his eyes. He seems sincere enough, but I wonder if he isn't just playing a role. Then he motions for us to sit down across from an oversized mahogany desk. "Do you have your husband's clothes for the service?" Mr. Rubin asks. Mom hands him the box. He opens a large, three-ring notebook with a black cover that has plastic-covered pages.

"I understand how difficult it is to discuss this now, but I want to show you the options you have for your husband for an appropriate service."

He passes the large book to us. Mom and I leaf through the pages. Each page displays a price on the top, ranging from two thousand to fourteen thousand dollars, and a list of options for coffins, flowers and the arrangements. "I want to make this as easy as possible in your time of bereavement," Mr. Ruben says somewhat insincerely.

"My husband said he didn't want an expensive funeral," Mom counters. She has her finger on the two thousand dollar page. Maybe Mr. Rubin can see that Mom isn't so far gone that she is going to drop a bundle of money here. I imagine most widows are ready to have Mr. Rubin choose the whole thing for them. I sense Mom's antennae going up about "being taken."

"I'd like to show you our viewing room. Then you can actually see the caskets, and choose one that you like," he says as he gets up. This meeting must be the same one he has had several times a day for years. I marvel at his efforts at sincerity, as if we are the only ones who have ever lost a husband and a father. It must get very tiring doing this job every day, I reflect.

He ushers us into a large, cream-colored room filled with open caskets displayed on shelves much like a staircase with deep risers. There are also open caskets on the floor in the center of the room. The contrast between the cream-colored walls and the dark wood caskets creates a serene mood. I hear the strands of "Embraceable You" from large speakers hanging from corners near the ceiling. It is calming.

We walk down each aisle, looking inside each casket. On top of the silk lining of each box is a large, clear plastic-covered card, with the price and funeral options.

"I will leave you alone to look for now. You'll find the prices inside," says Mr. Rubin, and we are left to browse comfortably. "What do you think of this one, Dear?" Mom asks.

We peer into a mahogany wood box with a dusty pink and lavender silk interior covering the inside of the open lid and cushioning the bottom and sides of the coffin.

I whisper, "It looks too Gentile." Mom nods in agreement. We move on.

"Can you believe these prices?" I say, as I look at a casket that is priced at eight thousand dollars.

"I was just thinking, maybe there might be some sale items," Mom says absentmindedly. We laugh. I know that Mom is always on the lookout for a bargain. It strikes us both as funny that her antennae are up even in this situation.

"This sure feels like shopping to me," I giggle.

Then we spot a casket made of maple, with a simple, cream-colored lining. "He would like this one," Mom says. At that moment, I spy a plain pine box with a Jewish star on it.

"How about this one? It's pretty simple."

"That's the kind of coffin that Orthodox are buried in," Mom says. "They wrap the body in a white shroud. No, that wouldn't work."

"It's too plain for Dad, I guess," I respond.

Mr. Rubin enters quietly and walks towards us on the plush gray rug. He asks, "So, what did you find?"

"I think this four thousand dollar maple wood one would work." Mom says to Mr. Rubin, while looking over for my approval.

"Good choice," Mr. Rubin says. "We can go with that one."

"How about putting a Jewish star on top, like on the pine box over there?" Mom requests.

"Okay, we can do that. No problem," Mr. Rubin answers. Mom and Mr. Rubin discuss the funeral arrangements while I bring the car around to the front of the mansion. It is to be a simple ceremony at the temple with Rabbi Gruen presiding early the next day, and then we will go on to the cemetery in Kenilworth, New Jersey, about forty minutes from the temple.

By the time Mom is in the car, she is geared up again. "We have to stop at Tabotchnick's to pick up cold cuts for the people that will be coming to the house this afternoon to pay their respects. We have to feed them."

Tabotchnick's Delicatessen, clothes shopping and praying at temple are hard-wired together as a spiritual experience in my psyche.

Wandering through the racks of dresses and trying on clothes in the fitting rooms of Orbachs, Hahnes, Bamberger's, and later when we had more money, Lord & Taylor and Saks Fifth Avenue, was where my relationship with Mom grew, deepened and ripened over the years. Of course, there were good years and rocky years.

In junior high, I wanted skirts that were tight and sexy. My idea of attractiveness was Marilyn Monroe; Mom's was Doris Day. She often won, but not without a fight. Then there were moments of sweetness, like the day I couldn't stop weeping in the Bamberger's fitting room, surrounded by large- breasted saleswomen. One announced that I was still too small to own a bra. Mom bent down, embraced me and said, *"Nin s'vet dir gornisht helfen* (it's not beyond help)," and ordered the salesgirl to find me a padded bra.

Mom's shopping lessons were a mixture of intimacy and practical advice. She would decide that I needed a Black Watch plaid skirt for school. She'd find one and turn it inside out to examine how it was made. If it was made poorly, she would mutter, *"shmatta"* (rag), and throw it back in the pile on the table. If she found something she liked, she would say, "You could use this, you could get a lot of wear out of this." She would carry it around in her arms until she dragged from the weight of all the outfits she had collected. Finally a salesgirl would put the collection in a fitting room.

One of my many shopping lessons was in goal-setting. Once Mom set her mind to something, she ruthlessly went through every rounder and bargain bin until she found it. Then we'd traipse from store to store comparing prices until we found the best quality and price. In this, she taught me to focus on what I wanted and snatch it, a metaphor for life. "Grab what you like now. Don't waste time trying it on until you have enough. If you wait, it will be gone," she would yell at me, as I meandered in back of the rounders of teens' twin sets, close behind in her search for the perfect Black Watch skirt.

I would dream of having large breasts like Francine Tenenbaum. I saw myself in a pink twin set like Sandra Dee kissing Frankie Avalon on the beach, Natalie Wood embracing James Dean in *Rebel Without a Cause*, or Linda Pastow, my girlfriend, who already had a handsome, wealthy boyfriend in college. But Mom had very distinct ideas of what a thirteen-year-old girl should wear: saddle shoes, twirl skirts, bows and ankle socks. In my mother's book, my thoughts were subversive.

After shopping, a consuming hunger would set in. We'd stop at Tabotchnick's Deli on the way home.

We'd meet Dad at exactly six o'clock, as the manager ushered us out of the closing store. Dad's brand new 1955 Chevy smelled of stale cigarette smoke. He drove home through the back streets of Newark to a little alley where Tabotchnick's had once been located. The sun was low on the horizon.

"This is where I grew up. We played stoopball here, on Billy Blaunick's stoop." He'd point out the house as we turned the corner onto Broom Street. Dirty brick tenements lined street after street. Garbage pails overflowed on each curb.

"Roll up the window! Close the window!" Mom would scream.

Harry and I would stop punching each other and look out the window at black people sitting outdoors on the steps of their homes, even on the coldest winter days. Things had really changed since Dad came over on the boat from Tanapole with his mother. When my ex-husband boasted to my mom that his family came over on the boat, she silenced him by responding, "OUR family came over on a plane." They remained wary of one another after that. "Saul, get out of this neighborhood. The children, the children!" My mother would yell. I picked up her fear, and wondered how she could work unafraid in the ghetto during the week, but on weekends, with her family, fear for her life in this neighborhood.

Tobotchnick's was down one alley. We jumped out of the car and odors of fish, just like the smell of the seashore, filled my nostrils. Set out on tables made of wooden saw horses and doors, were whole smoked salmon, sturgeon, whitefish, bagels, fresh rye, pumpernickel and crusty white bread.

Fat Jewish men with aprons tied around their bellies scurried around yelling, hawking, ridiculing and joking with the customers. The scales and fat from the fish lay on the black asphalt beneath the makeshift plywood tables. Cats of all sizes and shapes darted around, fighting for the fish carcasses.

I crouched under the tables to pet the kittens from the feral cats and tomcats that roamed the alleys at night. If I couldn't have a kitten of my own, I'd make friends with one here.

Dad haggled over the price of a piece of whitefish while he kept one eye on me. "Honey, don't pet the cats. You'll put your fingers in your mouth and get sick," he would tell me.

"Mr. Tabotchnick and Sadie moved to the suburbs after the Newark riots in the Sixties. The location may have changed, but not much else has," Mom says as I pull into the parking lot off of Springfield Avenue. In front of me is a huge, glass-windowed storefront. The Tabatchnick's of today is in a strip mall, with plastic tables and chairs. A large picture window is plastered with their specials of the day: Gefilte Fish, Kishka, Whitefish Sale.

It feels strange being so close to St. Barnabas Hospital and not seeing Dad. An emptiness fills my stomach. I look over at Mom, who is sitting there quietly, smaller and frailer than I remember her a week, a day or even an hour ago. Her skin seems so delicate and translucent. I see blue veins in her bare arms.

I look down at her hands and notice the narrowness of her fingers. Fingers that look like a seven-year-old's. Can this be my mother? Is this the same woman I knew growing up? Parents don't die. They are like sunsets and sunrises — predictable. You can always find them in the same place. When I was seven, she seemed so ample, so formidable.

Opening the door to the deli, I catch the overpowering odor of garlic pickling brine and fish. The glass counter displays cases of smoked sturgeon, bagels, various kinds of smoked salmon, a barrel of briny water filled with kosher pickles, and all kinds of shmears: cream cheese with lox, chives, fruit, herring and caviar.

A short, stout old man with an unshaven face and a stained white apron tied low around his belly comes out from behind the counter. "What'll ya have?" he barks.

Mom stands on her toes and lifts her arms so that her hands touch the top of the counter and her face is at the level of the old man's. Her purse dangles from her forearm. "Give me two pounds of lox, not salty, same with sturgeon and whitefish. I want two dozen bagels and two cinnamon babka. Oh, before you get the whitefish, give me a taste, so I know what I am getting. I want your best, not fatty."

He gives her a disgusted look, the one he reserves for people who are picky, and wipes his hands on his grimy white apron. "Lady! Ai-Ai-Ai, here's a *bissel* (a little) for a taste. Fatty schmatty. Don't you trust me? Our business is as old as dirt. You new in the neighborhood?"

Mom doesn't back off, but she seems self-conscious as she tries to make herself appear bigger by stretching on her toes. She giggles anxiously. "I've lived here for forty years. You're the new one in the neighborhood! I just don't want my guests to complain that I'm not a good hostess," she continues flirtatiously, putting the blame graciously back on herself. Mom, the consummate diplomat with men — they love her. She wheedles, she maneuvers, not that she would call it that.

The storekeeper smiles. She has made a friend.

I stand behind her.

"Wanna sandwich, we have some tasty specials," Tabotchnick, says.

She turns toward me. "Want a sandwich before we go back to the house?" she asks.

"Do we have time?"

"Sure, Denny can't come, but Helen, Abe, Moe, Gilda and Rhonda will be there. Harry should be arriving soon and has the key to open the door for them. This won't take long."

I go back to the counter and order a turkey sandwich with mustard on fresh, dark rye. Mom follows me and orders the same thing except with a kosher new pickle that she picks out by sticking her hand deep into the briny barrel near the door.

Mom is wiping her hands on a paper napkin when she sits down across from me at the plastic table by the window. "I am so angry at Harry," Mom says. "He is so mean." She says this with a little-girl pout on her face. "I was telling him about how Mrs. Rhinehardt was left a widow. She was having a hard time remembering things, so she gave her daughter power of attorney and put her in charge of her money. Well, the old lady almost starved to death, because her daughter refused to give her cash for food. She was a prisoner in her own house."

I remembered the Rhinehardts as an old couple who had a fenced-in driveway that housed a barking German shepherd. The kids on the block were afraid to play near their house because of the dog. "Mom, remember when Dad said they had stick furniture and hardwood floors with scatter rugs? He said Jews have comfortable furniture and wall-to-wall carpets," I laugh, sharing a piece of old times. It feels good to bring up his name.

Mom smiles.

"Harry's behavior reminds me of the Rhinehardts. I'm afraid he will do the same thing to me. If I am incompetent, just pull the plug."

I put my sandwich down. Suddenly, I'm not very hungry.

"Mom, you have a rich life ahead: places to go and people to see and things to do. You aren't planning to die anytime soon, are you?" I ask her.

"No, Dear, I hope not!" Mom says reassuringly. "I am just telling you this so that you know. I don't want any life support like Dad. Just let me die."

I wonder if she felt that keeping Dad alive had been a mistake, but I am afraid to ask her. I sense that if she really felt that way, she would get angry with me instead of copping to it.

"Pull the plug?" I ask, trying to make light of it.

"Pull the plug!" she says dramatically. We laugh at the finality of her words and eat our deli sandwiches in silence.

Kids are playing stoopball as we turn into our street. A neighbor at the end of the block is trimming her rose bushes. She looks up and waves. Apparently, the word hasn't gotten around yet.

Our white clapboard house stands high on a red brick porch, like a pedestal surrounded by a postage stamp of lawn, within spitting distance of the houses on either side. This subdivision was built right after the war. A towering oak tree grows in the backyard. It is the only one of any size on the block.

I spot some plants on the lawn that look exactly like cabbage and turn to Mom as we pull in the driveway. "What is that stuff sprouting up on the borders?" I ask.

"Oh, dear, isn't that lovely. It's called cabbage. It's a hardy border trim."

Mom's taste often confounds me. The cabbage as border trim makes her lawn look like Old Macdonald's roadside farm.

Harry's Taurus and Uncle Moe and Aunt Gilda's Lincoln Town Car are parked in the front of the house. Mom's distant cousin Rhonda's little Jetta is parked in the driveway by the garage. I am bracing myself for receiving relatives I haven't seen in quite awhile. Mom is usually the gracious hostess, my ambassador and ally, smoothing over any of my thoughtless transgressions — like inadvertently asking Gilda about something that is off limits to discuss in the family.

"You like my cabbages as decoration?" Mom says.

"Sure," I answer. "Do many rabbits come by?"

"*A nar vakst on regen* (a fool grows without rain)," Mom retorts.

I smile because she has dished it back, and I know she was talking about me.

12

"Midnight at the Oasis, don't take your camel to bed," filled the solarium as Rick and I effortlessly glided over the parquet floor to the amusement and laughter of his family. In this insular Cape Code mansion on a humid June evening in 1973, we clung, leaving no spaces between us, while he quietly hummed the words in my ear. I felt his long eyelashes bewitch me deep inside my skin. He was an itch that wouldn't go away. Each word conveyed our own special meaning, and the promise of lovemaking later, when we disappeared upstairs, finally alone.

I felt the curious indentation in the middle of his chest, a birth defect, of his otherwise perfect Episcopalian tall and wiry body, while his shoulders, broad and square, held him erect and made him look like royalty. I swam in his aqua-blue eyes and wanted to rest in his nest of thick silvery hair, a premature seasoning to such a young chiseled face. He didn't know what it did to me, this half man, half woman-looking body, and I left it that way. I am a Virgo — cool and calculating.

We tried to teach his mom and dad the new craze, the Bump, to "Rock the Boat." I patiently waited for his mother and father, older brother Lipson and Suzette, Lipson's wife and my graduate program advisor, to go up to bed. Lipson had introduced us against Suzette's protests. Rick's recent ex-wife, Muffy Jo, and Suzette were not only close friends, but they grew up together in the deep South and were southern belles through and through.

Then we made our way upstairs to his childhood room and made love until we were spent. Afterwards, we whispered secrets to each other in the early dark hours of the morning.

When Rick was seven, his mom and dad sent him off alone on a long train ride with only his little suitcase labeled Camp Red Dog. He traveled for hundreds of miles alone and bereft, in the hands of a strange conductor. I imagined that indentation was the wound unhealed in his heart, as the train drew farther and farther away from his mother. I told him about my coming home to the empty house. We shared our abandonment and that made us whole for a while. He told me that his mother had a nervous breakdown when he was eleven and had to be hospitalized with shock treatment. She returned several months later a different person. His twin sister died of anorexia nervosa two years later.

He spoke of his unsatisfying marriage to Muffy Jo, and what it felt like to try to conceive a child and fail. She put him on a schedule of intercourse and her control made the love fly out of the relationship. They adopted a child, half Cherokee. Nine months later, she conceived their first son. Then she found out that Rick went to prostitutes. He said he had no choice. She left him.

Now, I try to remember what it was about him, as I look at a photo of him sitting on a bench in Beacon Hill Park. On either side are his two boys, six and eight years old, smiling and jumping up, caught by the eye of the camera in mid-air, just before they land hard on the bench. But I only see Rick. I never really looked at the children in the picture until after it was all over. If anyone had asked me about the photo, I would have said it was a picture of just Rick.

The sound track to my arrival at the University of Massachusetts was "Chariots of Fire." After a grueling trip across country, I drove into the center of the small New England town late on an August afternoon. Humidity hung thick in the overcast sky, East-Coast style. I parked my car up on the curb and ran in to get a sandwich. I was several days late for my scheduled arrival and meeting with my dissertation advisor, Dr. Suzette Lewis.

When I returned, an Amherst police officer was just writing me a ticket. "I don't know where you get off parking on the sidewalk. You might get away with that where you come from," he said as he motioned towards my personalized California license plates, "but here we park in designated areas." If I had been smart, I might have taken this as my first cue, that I was just a guest in this state, an outsider, and should remember my place, but I didn't.

"I have heard so many wonderful things about you and your Gestalt Art Therapy Groups," said Suzette in her silky southern way of drawing out words, when I finally found her house on the woody outskirts of the campus. It was more like a California mansion — open with glass and chrome and shag rugs. Her husband, Lipson Johnson Lewis, a tall, graying, attractive man, greeted me warmly, pipe in mouth. If this is what having a doctor's degree confers on you, I thought, I want some. They seemed so stable, sophisticated and mature — a portrait of a happily married couple. Something I couldn't achieve. So far my scorecard was Marriage 1, Divorce 1.

"We've spent some time down at Esalen, and love the weather and the workshops. You're so lucky to actually live there," Lipson said as we drank tea and ate cookies their black maid served us.

He noticed me looking. In these parts there were few people of color.

"I want you to meet Chantelle, she's been with us since I was a child," Suzette explained. "Chantelle was given to me as a wedding gift from my family, and was a wet nurse for my two baby daughters. Now that Chantelle is getting old, and she's not very bright," Suzette lowered her voice to a whisper, "she is slowly being relieved of her duties." Apparently, tea was still one of them.

God, it felt good to be part of a family, but I was confused about Chantelle. I thought slavery went out with Abraham Lincoln. Although my mom and dad were only four hours away via the Connecticut Turnpike, I was too busy falling in love with Suzette, Lipson, and what Christian families do, think, eat and wear to think of them.

Suzette took a special interest in me, being so far away from home, she said. But I think I was a bit of an oddity: Jewish, energetic, single, a California-type. My entertainment value was high during the bleak winters in Amherst. Since I was in Suzette's core group, we drove to Rhode Island each week and back as part of the Artists in the Schools program.

Suzette began to confide in me. "The travel agent called my sister in law, Muffy Jo, with her seat assignment for a week-end flight to Toronto with her husband. Rick was flying out of town that weekend alone on business, but the agent said he had booked a flight for Mr. and Mrs. Lewis. She was certain the agent had made a mistake. Well, you can imagine. That bastard was taking another woman away for the weekend and lying to Muffy Jo. Lipsie and I only suspected all these years. Poor Muffy Jo and their two little babies. She wants a divorce!"

For the next two years, we fell into a kind of groove. Suzette, Lipson, their daughters and I shared a lot of confidences. They went through my anguish about not being able to meet the right man and my pain over a chiropractor I met at the local growth center who was fifteen years my senior. He wanted me to look like his estranged wife. He was encouraging me to straighten my hair and dye it blond. They put their foot down.

This guy lived near Lipson's mother and father in Hartford. So that Easter, Lipson brought Rick, who lived in Beacon Hill, over to meet me at my boyfriend's house while he was away straightening out financial things with his estranged wife. When Suzette found out Rick had met me, she was furious at Lipson, because her first loyalty was to Muffy Jo, and so it drove a wedge into their marriage as well.

Rick and I became inseparable after his divorce. Each weekend he would drive to Amherst or I'd visit him at his eagle's nest condo atop Beacon Hill.

Lipson was surprisingly happy that his younger brother and I were an item. Lipson was in his mid-forties, hating his life in Amherst, having a lot of time on his hands and wanting some adventure in his marriage. His two girls were growing up fast and moving out into the world.

One afternoon on a walk through campus, he told me about his adventures with Suzette at a sex club in Manhattan. "My brother sees prostitutes, so do I — male and female," he told me. "Rick was seeing this woman who worked as a psychologist during the day, and at night she was a high-class call girl. He wanted to fall in love with her, but she told him to bug off. The woman he went to Canada with was blue-collar. My folks didn't like his dating out of his class."

This prostitute thing made the boys all the more interesting to me. I had never met a man who openly talked about seeing prostitutes. I also wondered about the blue-collar girl. How would their parents feel about a Jewish girl, and worse, how would my parents feel?

I broached the subject. My mother became hysterical. "You are going to convert? Is that it? He will want you to convert! A goy, we send you to come home a diploma and you come home a Christian?"

"No Mom, I'm not converting. I promise. Besides, he hasn't even asked me to marry him. You want me to marry a doctor? I'm tired of waiting for the doctor. If I wait any longer, I'm going to become one."

By this time school was ending, and I only had to write my dissertation. No more classes. I could do this anywhere, but I wanted to do it in Rick's arms. Sure, his kids were a pain in the ass, but I overlooked their existence, just the way I failed to see them in the photo he gave me.

One weekend I was over at his place and the kids were there. Bert, his oldest, saw me typing and asked me, "What are you doing?"

"I'm writing my dissertation, I'm going to become a doctor one day," I said proudly, using this moment as a feminist learning lesson for the next generation of males.

He looked up at me with his clear brown eyes and said, "Gee, that looks like office work to me. My mom was an airline hostess. She flew with real pilots, not clerical work like you."

And then there were his parents. His mother, intrusive in her Lillie Pulitzer outfits and Papagallo flats, and I was bored by their endless cocktail parties, double martinis, and all those Daughter of the American Revolution relatives we were called upon to pay a social call.

I was swept away with this sociological research into the life and times of a Boston Brahmin family. I was learning so much in my counseling program at school and from seeing it in action on weekends at their exclusive compound outside of Hyannis. Their patterns of communications, family dynamics, dysfunctional, non-verbal gestures, like smiling when they were angry, their projections, and transference fascinated me. The way they furnished their compound on Cape Cod with stick furniture and throw rugs intrigued me. It was just like Dad had observed with the Rhinehardts, our neighbors across the street. I had my own action field research in my own backyard. The Lewises were far more interesting than my own family.

After one evening meal while we were cleaning up the kitchen, Rick commented to Lipson, Suzette and me "Did you see how angry Dad was tonight?" I looked at their three faces in disbelief. "He didn't scream or shout or even raise his voice, how could you tell he was angry?" I asked incredulously.

Lipson whispered so Chantelle couldn't hear us in the next room. "It was how he shifted in his seat. Didn't you see that!"

"Oh, my God, he was angry," Suzette agreed. "He got upset when someone mentioned Muffy's name in front of Rick."

At the dinner table as elsewhere, there were several grown women who had doctoral degrees, while their spouses didn't, but our opinions were minimized and discounted by old Mr. Lewis. In my immigrant family, the women ruled the roost, but I came to see that in this Mayflower-migrated family it was "father knows best." Once I crossed Rick's father on a political issue and he gave me the silent treatment for months.

It was the first time in my life that I became aware of how other families expressed emotions. My doctoral studies were indeed paying off.

I was graduating. I was going to become a psychologist with a doctor's degree, and I had nowhere to go. I hadn't planned the next step in my life. One weekend before Thanksgiving, Rick and I ran off and got married in matching J. Crew white sweaters and topsiders. His parents offered to take us on a honeymoon to Bermuda. What I didn't realize was they meant themselves, Rick's two kids, Lipson and Suzette and their two kids — along with us. So we honeymooned for two weeks as a family of ten. I was so co-opted by the sheer momentum of this family that I just went along, not understanding or knowing what I wanted. I was just so grateful to be rescued by a family, not my own. A family of means.

Would I become a Boston Brahmin also? I entertained pictures of myself as a Kennedy type as I sat next to Rick at the wheel of Big Bertha, his forty-five foot red power boat and we hammered our way over the white caps from Cape Cod to Martha's Vineyard. We were taking his kids on board to buy ice cream cones. "These cones cost about fifty dollars each," he joked as he turned and swooped into his own private dock while hundreds of tourists watched us from the shore.

When I finally told my parents (after all, they wanted me to assimilate), they did the only dignified thing they could do. They called his parents and were invited up to the Hartford Estate to meet Mr. and Mrs. Lewis for dinner. Mom was decked out in her Gucci bag and shoes. Dad wore his best suit. They looked small and scared, like they were meeting the lion in his den. Later they sent Mrs. Lewis a thank-you note:

> *Dear Mildred,*
> *Thank you for entertaining us at your lovely home. We enjoyed meeting you and Mr. Lewis, and spending the afternoon with your beautiful grandchildren.*
> *We hope when you are down our way, you will come for dinner.*
> *Our best to you and the children,*
> *Sarah (Mr. and Mrs. Saul Perlman)*

What dreams did I get swept up in? Our closeness was short-lived. When Muffy Jo heard that we married, she punished Rick in a way that only she could. She took the kids and moved back to Macon, Georgia.

Rick was dumbstruck. The fun went out of our lives. He sat at home after work, depressed, cut-off and mute. He hid behind newspapers, magazines and sleep. He stopped talking to me. I became the culprit.

"Talk to me," I shouted. It was useless. The more I fought to have him open up, the more he held a grudge towards me. He wouldn't forgive me for one transgression before I made another one.

After six months of this, Lipson called me one day. "You ought to know that Rick is planning on moving out. He was just going to get a truck and leave you with an empty house. I couldn't let him do that, so I wanted to tell you."

But Lipson was too late. That afternoon, I put the key in the lock and walked into a vacant apartment. All our wedding gifts and furniture were gone. My marriage was over. I was left with what I came into the marriage with — nothing but dreams. My doctoral degree was left untouched on the empty wall in the study. My mother and father were so disgusted with me by that time, they had nothing left to say.

Years later, Lipson visited me in San Francisco. This was long after he had divorced Suzette and his daughter had committed suicide. Chantelle was in an institution for handicapped people, and his mom and dad had passed away.

"You were so smart to leave when you did," he said. "You saw how messed up my family was. Rick lives in Fairfield, Connecticut, now. Muffy Jo moved back and they share the same home but live on separate floors, and each raises one of the kids. Rick dates, but Muffy Jo doesn't."

"I wasn't smart," I said. "I was just caught up. I didn't have a plan after I graduated, so when in doubt, I got married!" We both chuckled, and he put his arm around me and kissed the top of my head. That was the last I saw of him. Several years later, I read about him in the *New York Times* Obituary section. He had died of AIDS. They had written nice things about his work at the college, and it mentioned that his department chair was empty. My dad always said, the obituaries are the best place to find a new job.

13

Early the next morning, the family meets at B'nai Shof-far. Rabbi Gruen ushers Mom and me into a small room and gives us a torn black ribbon to wear. He explains, "This is the Hebrew symbol of mourners who tear their clothes into shreds in grief." Then he asks Mom if she wants the casket open or closed.

"I want to see Saul first. Then you can close the casket," she says stoically. Her mood has changed since yesterday. Her face is drawn and tired.

The rabbi pins a black ribbon onto the lapel of each member of the family in a slow, silent ritual. Mom, Harry, Uncle Moe, Francine, Roberta and I file into the small chapel to view the body. Harry hangs back with Roberta and Francine. I can't understand why he does that. Maybe he just can't bear to see Dad now.

In a four thousand dollar casket from Bernstein's lies a man barely resembling my dad. I peer in to view an old man with eyes that look like glass in a waxen body. His body is spongy to my touch. His face is painted a pastel green-blue hue. I have heard that cosmetology students-in-training are often called in by morticians to practice on dead people. This crosses my mind as I look at his blush colored lips.

"This doesn't look like Dad. It looks like someone they took from a shelf. Let's supply them a Jewish man in his eighties," I quip. I feel disappointed and let down.

Mom frowns. "Oh, Honey," she says softly. She seems to be consoling both of us. The others file in. "Well, at least he wore his new suit," Mom whispers to me.

Solemnly, Rabbi Gruen ushers us into the first row of the small chapel. We squeeze into the pew and sit stiffly on the wooden seats. I feel the warmth of Mom's body next to me. The people that Dad knew best sit up front: Uncle Moe, Aunt Clara, Aunt Helen, Roberta, Harry, Francine, Mom and me. I want Dad to have a grand funeral in the big sanctuary. I hadn't anticipated this small turnout.

Dad comes from a generation when men didn't have male friends. "My wife is my best friend," I often heard him tell her when she wanted him to be more "social," as she called it. He scoffed at my husband's male support groups. "Male bonding," he said. "Doesn't the man have a wife to talk to?" I always thought it was the source of his depression. After working all day and taking care of his wife and two kids, maybe there wasn't much left over.

I wonder if these people are friends that Mom has made. I don't know some of them. In the last few decades of his life, Dad had withdrawn more and more.

Mom would get angry when I probed into her life with Dad: "Did you ever sleep apart? What's the worst argument you both ever had? What was sex like the first time?"

"I could *plotz* from such questions! Why do you ask questions like these?" she used to say. "When you come home I feel like we are part of a family therapy session."

I had only wanted to get an understanding of what marriage was really like. I wondered if we shared some common feelings as women about similar episodes.

The rabbi opens the small sanctuary. It smells cool and musty from disuse. He walks to the far corner of the vast darkness and switches on the lights. They come up softly. The gold of the ark, the mahogany of the *bema* create a brilliance to the room. It is a formidable space.

On the plane I had written a eulogy for my dad. I had thought I was prepared, but now I'm not so sure. What can I say about him? I shift in the wooden pew. My eulogy has to be about him. How I have criticized the eulogies by people in other funerals, where I learned more about the person speaking than about the deceased! Are we all just reflections in the eyes of another person?

It is a brief and formal ceremony. First the rabbi speaks, then Harry gives a prepared speech. There he stands, wooden and self-conscious reading his speech from the pulpit — a long and formal testimony to Dad. Mom whispers to me, "Roberta told me he practiced in the car all the way up here." It is a four-hour drive from Maryland.

When fourteen-year-old Francine's turn comes to speak, she remains planted in her seat. After much whispering between her and her mother, Roberta bounces up to the pulpit instead. "My daughter asked me to give her speech," she says to the audience. And so she begins reading from the crumpled paper Francine has handed her.

"My grandfather loved to hear me play my Casio piano while he played his violin with me. He used to say, after he and Grandma Sarah bought me a new dress, 'Wear it in good health.' I always thought that was funny," Roberta begins, and looks at the audience for approval.

Muffled laughter comes from the congregation. Roberta takes in the appreciation from the audience and basks in the attention. She wants her daughter to become an actress, but Francine is growing into a more introverted personality, like her dad.

Now it is my turn. I am feeling numb and unreal, but my legs are strangely energetic. They want to bound up there. I look out over the small gathering, feeling grateful after all for the small turnout. I want to speak from my heart, but my heart isn't talking. What can I say that isn't false or trite? I am dwelling on other, less suitable details for a eulogy.

I remember one weekend when I came home from college. I found him in the den. "I want to read you something," he said.

He was always sending me things he cut out of the newspapers. Things that had facts and data that substantiated his opinion about how women shouldn't have sex before marriage, or how women needed to honor their husbands, or why teaching was an honest profession. I often felt angry and rebellious after reading these, and I threw them out.

He read me a poem. I can't remember who wrote it, but it used a tree as a metaphor. It was like the oak tree out in our backyard. Towards the end I saw moisture forming in the seams of his eyes. I felt myself overcome with his emotion. We both were weeping, trying not to allow each other to recognize the love we had for each other.

I admitted it to myself. I'd been afraid of the electrical connection Dad and I had. It felt very sexual. Maybe he read this poem because he felt that I was growing up and slowly moving away.

In the shadows of my memory, I am napping on the brown and red plaid cotton hide-a-bed in the room that Harry and I share. Dad's arms are wrapped around my five-year-old body. He feels warm and protective. Suddenly, Mom's voice jars us awake. "Saul, get up and help me. *Aroysgevorfen* (thrown out and wasted time)! Don't sleep the afternoon away!"

He turns over. "Just a half an hour more."

I start crying. "Daddy, Daddy, don't let her boss you around."

"You said you'd help me. I can't clean the house alone. It's too much. I need your help."

Dad's on his feet. I'm cold and jarred from the warm protective world of my Dad and me.

"Leave him alone. You ought to divorce her. She's a witch!" I yell in her face.

She won't slap me when he's around. I can feel that I've said something important. He is being swayed. I can feel him move his dense frame towards me. Then something changes in him.

"Don't talk to your mother that way!" He moves away from me. I had him for a moment, but then the circuitry was broken.

Years later, my mom told me how I withdrew from them. "You used to be so cuddly. Suddenly you stopped jumping into our bed or hugging us. I've always wondered what happened."

I felt betrayed by my father and resentful of my mom. I feared her hard edges.

I was Electra in Clytemnestra's home. It was only after I married that I was safe. Mom moved closer and Dad relaxed with me. I wanted my father too much, and because she was shrewd, my mother knew it. Mom was just protecting her man, a primitive emotion.

I only tell the good parts of his life today in the sanctuary, not how incapable he was of giving the kind of love a child needed, how frightened a man he was, how difficult it was for him to make friends with people, how willful and vindictive he was at times, how difficult his life was or, how he hated his work. How he would have been a musician if he had thought more of himself. How he settled in life because he fell in love with my mother and they had kids. How he sacrificed his dreams for us, and we turned out not to be the way he'd planned.

"My dad encouraged me to be an artist, because he was filled with music he couldn't express."

A procession led by the hearse with Dad's coffin and flanked by two New Jersey motorcycle police drives slowly down to Beth David Memorial Park in Kenilworth, where Dad will be buried. "It was the strangest thing to go shopping for funeral plots with Dad," Mom tells me in the limo.

I agree. "It's like buying tires. You know it's essential, but it isn't a purchase you get a lot of pleasure out of."

The cemetery is in an industrial section of town. Tall, rectangular warehouses stand on all three corners. On the fourth corner is a gravel driveway leading to a fenced-in half acre of land, surrounded a swampy meadow and an industrial park.

"You know, Dear, they are building a Nordstrom about ten minutes away from here," Mom turns to me to tell me. She knows we might come here and shop together, and later visit Dad.

Half a dozen people from the temple are at the cemetery. The ceremony is brief. I notice there is an empty plot next to Dad for Mom. I wonder what she is thinking at that moment. There's a stoic look to her body, and her eyes look down into the grave. The gravediggers are dressed in workmen's clothes and stand a respectable distance away, waiting to fill the grave.

The sun creates a cloudless Jersey sky. Rabbi Gruen says a Hebrew prayer as they lower Dad into the ground. He throws a handful of dirt onto the casket. It makes a dull, hard thumping sound as it hit my dad's box. Dirt on my dad's body. My dad who was so meticulous. I feel empty as we walk back to the car, over the carpet of thick, manicured grass.

On the ride home, Mom is sitting next to me in the back seat. "You know, we probably have stuff from yesterday to warm up for people coming over. They'll be hungry. Some of the other girls are bringing casseroles."

She is referring to the group of women friends she made over the years at Avalon Avenue School, the ghetto school she worked at, and old friends from her nursing days waiting at home.

As we enter the back door, I can feel a festive air. Rhonda has arrived earlier and set the large wooden dining room table with Mom's best china, silverware and plates. Rhonda kisses Mom on the cheek, and then gives me a peck too. Then she grabs our bags and begins opening and laying out the food we bought.

"Did you take the plastic off the chairs and sofa?" asks Mom.

"Yes, yes, yes. Did you get any mustard?" Rhonda asks back.

Mom shakes her head. "*Oy*, I forgot. Let's see if there's some in the pantry." She disappears and reappears with a yellow plastic mustard jar.

The tiny living room is already crowded with neighbors. I recognize the two young people who bought the Hamiltons' house, next door. They are talking to my brother.

"Beverly and Jay Humbarg are born-again Christians," Mom told me in a phone conversation. They look out of place on this warm and balmy evening. They wear topsiders and khaki baggy pants. Very preppy for this crowd. Mom thinks they are nice, helpful people, despite their religion.

It always felt unusual to have a non-Jew in our house. My parents taught me that the world was divided into two categories: Jews and Goyim. The Jews were the chosen people. Jews read books, got educated and made money. They were successful. Goys drank, had fun and belonged to private clubs.

Roberta and Francine, Harry's wife and daughter, sit on the sofa. Uncle Moe and Aunt Gilda sit several yards away, but they are not talking to anyone. They sit erect and inert, and they look uncomfortable. They've had a rocky relationship with my mom for many years. Maybe they attended out of duty.

Mom is running around in the kitchen, getting the food ready with Rhonda. The doorbell rings constantly. Mom, wiping her hands on her apron, runs to the front door each time.

I feel very protective of her. I want to be alone with her. I want to hug and comfort her, but she keeps hosting. I'm afraid she will wear herself out.

"I can get the door, Mom," I say.

"Oh, no. I want to greet my guests." And each time the door rings, she comes running out again.

The living room is filling up with relatives: Loretta and Mehuda, Rhonda's mother's sister, Mandy Dresden, a woman who works as a volunteer at the temple, Edith Graft, Anne Steinberg — women my mom's age. The people feel so familiar. When I was a kid, Mom and Dad gave parties. I would sit on the landing and listen to their chatter. Today feels strange, because although Dad's portrait hangs over the little fireplace, we will never see or hear from him again. Something inside my heart lurches each time I think of that.

The portrait of Dad was bought from a Sears and Roebuck photography salesman several Christmases ago. He got a thirty-six by thirty-six simulated oil painting portrait with a frame to hang over the fireplace, and one hundred small duplicates.

Harry had called it a portrait of "our founder" when he first encountered it hanging over the fireplace. It really didn't capture Dad at all, but I guess he was flattered by the full head of hair. For several years, Dad handed out those photo portraits to everyone he knew, telling them about the great deal he got at Sears. I thought it was funny. It really began as Mom's idea, but Dad began to enjoy it.

David arrives. He merges into the crowd after he drops his carry-on near the door. I am relieved to see him. Soon I can share the burden of the day alone with him. He looks tired. While I carry his stuff upstairs to my old bedroom, he hugs my mom and gets something to eat.

When I come back down, I find him talking and laughing with my brother Harry and my cousin Denny. David has always been wary of Harry, because of his strange silences, but he doesn't let that affect his social veneer.

Mom walks by and says, "What are you guys laughing about?" They don't answer.

"So, Sarah," says Denny, "When are you going to sell the house and move to a smaller place or to a retirement home?"

My mother bristles. "I haven't decided what I want to do."

Harry jumps in, "You could probably get two hundred thousand for this place, then get into a retirement home with the money. Everything would be taken care of until you die. You know they require an entrance fee these days." He turns to Denny. "I have all the papers drawn up, but she doesn't want to sign them. Maybe you can convince her."

David and I back away quietly. I don't like how this conversation is going. I wait to see what Mom will say.

She looks up at the large frame of Denny, the successful dry cleaner, and then she glances over at my brother. She seems to be assessing the situation. I know she is trying to be a good hostess and not offend anyone, but I can tell by her calm graciousness that she is really perturbed inside.

"Let's wait. We just buried Dad today. We have time." Stone-faced, Mom wipes her hands on her apron, turns and walks back into the kitchen.

I sit down on the couch. Exhaustion is seeping into my body. David hands me another glass of wine. It is my third one and I can feel myself getting sleepy. Roberta sits down beside me.

"You know, it is very difficult when someone dies," she says. "If they are a really great part of your life, their loss is devastating. You have so many memories of them, it is hard to put them aside. I know because I loved your father very much. I think it is important to grieve and show your emotions. Some people think emotions are to be controlled, but I think death is an important event."

I can feel my muscles ache and my blood begin to boil. How dare she lecture me? I am not a student of hers. I am older than she is. Has she forgotten how her own father died several years after Francine was born, and how her brother died right after that? Had she forgotten how after Francine was born, my mother and father had to take her away and care for her for two years while Roberta had a nervous breakdown? I am working overtime to control my tongue.

I can hear her voice drone on and on. I'm not listening to what she is saying. I only know when I look at that heavily made-up face, I want to strangle her.

Finally, I abandon all control of myself. The wine is my master. "I feel like you are lecturing me."

"Gee, I'm sorry," Roberta says blankly.

Now I can't stop myself.

"You know, my dad never liked you very much," I say. After years of holding it back, I feel relieved with this moment of truth-telling.

Her black eyes harden and her face reddens. "Oh, no. That isn't true. He loved me. I know that!" Roberta shrieks, jumps up and flounces into the kitchen. In that moment I hate myself, but I hate her more.

David wanders by then and makes a right into the den. I can hear the television droning on in the background. My mother turns around and starts to talk to some new arrivals. I follow David into the den.

"I gotta get outta here," he says. "I need some fresh air."
He is right. This is becoming a marathon.

"What do you want?" I ask, feeling like the other shoe is
going to drop.

"Let me take the car and go someplace by myself."

I feel the pain of abandonment shoot through my body, but
I know I can't control him. I don't want to make a scene. He'll
come back. I hand him the keys to Dad's car and he slips out.

That night David and I check into the Hilton up in Short
Hills. We order room service and lie in bed, watching an old
tape of Mohammed Ali being pummeled by Buster Johnson.
As we turn off the lights, David begins to massage my back;
soon I slip onto him softly and tenderly. In the background,
the in-house cable television channel is tuned into some sweet
violin music, and it lubricates our lovemaking. I see my dad
standing at the foot of the bed, playing his violin rocking on
his heels, as he sometimes did, and swaying at his knees and
hips. After the last climax, David rolls on his back and whispers
to me, "It seems like your dad paid us a visit." I nod, smiling,
and drift into a peaceful sleep. Dad has indeed paid me the
visit he promised, and I feel comforted by this one, unlike the
ones that followed.

14

Several nights later, back in California I receive a call from my mother.

"I just called to tell you how excited I am about my new adventure," she says.

"I called Mr. Hoffmeyer, the football coach at Columbia High School, and asked him if he could teach an old lady like me how to drive," she laughs. "He said he'd love to. So off I go tomorrow for my first driving lesson. If Dad could see me now!"

I smile on the other end of the phone, remembering that Mr. Hoffmeyer, the football coach, doubled as the driver education teacher, and he is still there after all these years. All the kids in Maplewood probably learned to drive from Mr. Hoffmeyer.

"If Dad could see you now!" I repeat. "He would take Mr. Hoffmeyer aside and read him the riot act! What's your first destination?"

"Well, he has to take me around the parking lot first to see that I won't destroy his car. Then I'll probably ask him to show me how to drive to my beauty parlor, and of course to Saks. So when you come home next time I can drive you there myself, and park," she adds.

"Parking would be a good thing," I quip.

"So how was your day, Dear?" she asks me.

I begin to tell her, feeling myself enjoy revealing every detail of my day. I move to the refrigerator and take out a bottle of Chardonnay, pull up a stool to the kitchen counter, reach for a glass from the shelf and pour myself a glass of wine. I picture Mom holding the receiver of the white rotary wall phone, sitting in the little wooden chair with the woven straw seat.

"Mom, you'll never guess what I found today. You'd be so proud of me," I chirp. David calls my conversations with my mother "chirping." We laugh, giggle, and chatter on in short, excited, choppy sentences.

"What, Dear?"

I have all of her attention. "Well, remember those Anne Klein II suits we saw at Macy's? I found them in Macy's here for half the price in petite six, and they fit perfectly."

My mom sounds elated. "You are such a good shopper," she says.

"Maybe when you come back, I can drive you around to the malls. By then I will know how to back out of the driveway. Actually, Mr. Hoffmeyer said that I'm pretty good. Do you have any tips for backing out of the driveway without taking the Humbargs' hedges with me?"

"Let's see. I usually focus on a spot in the middle of the street and head for that. Like a manhole cover, or something," I say.

"Oh, that's an idea. Harry said, if you want to go right, turn the wheel to the right, if you want to go left, turn the wheel to the left. Oh, I'll just practice. I'm sure dumber people than me have done this. I need to get around to my hair and nail appointments." I am pleased to hear Mom's old spunk coming back.

I think it must be a relief to finally let Dad go. Oh, I never could talk about it that way to Mom, but I know there must be some of that in her new energy. I feel that way. It was such a strain to see him deteriorating. I am afraid to ask her if it is a relief, she might get angry. Can she admit that to me? I am afraid she won't understand that I mean the ending to a bad situation, not that he died. When she flares up there is no discussing anything further, and she holds it against me, so I keep my mouth shut.

But her moods aren't always upbeat. Later that week, she sounds down.

"I'm just so tired sometimes," Mom says. I can sense it in her voice. "Harry never calls me, and when he does he is so abrupt with me, I just want to cry."

"I miss you, Mom," I respond. I want to take her in my arms right then and hug all the pain away. At the same time, I cherish her vulnerability. It is something she never really shared with me before, and it brings us closer. We really need each other now.

"Sunday nights are the loneliest," she continues. "During the day I can keep busy, but nights are really bad. Mrs. Nottingham is gone, and Mrs. Lynn's moved to Florida with her daughter. I'm the oldest living woman on this block."

I laugh. Even in my mother's sadness, I can hear her humor.

"I'll come back soon," I hear myself volunteering. In my heart, I ache for my mother, and feel like I just can't do enough. But in reality, I'm not sure I can ever do enough to satisfy my mom because she is so demanding.

"How about Father's Day?" Mom asks. "You and I could go to temple and then shopping. You know Saks has a summer sale that weekend."

When I was a child, summer mornings in New Jersey began with rising humidity in an overcast sky. By noon, the sun had penetrated the cloud cover. It was sweltering and the streets were deserted. With no warning, thunderstorms and lightning dramatically changed the mood of the day, darkening the landscape and canceling outdoor plans.

Those summers were intensely lonely, but held a strange beauty for me. The summer I was five years old, Mom, Harry and I spent July and August in a bungalow on the shores of Kiamesha Lake. Dad worked in the city and came up late on Friday nights to see us for the weekend.

I think we went back there because it was familiar. Mom grew up on a hill near the lake, and she first met Dad at a lake hotel where he was playing in the Bernie Perlman Band.

That particular summer day, the sky suddenly turned an ominous black. The air became very still, as if something supernatural was going to happen.

"Children, children!" Mom called frantically from the porch. A wind came up and in no time, buckets of rain came down, followed by a once-in-a-lifetime hurricane.

The leaves of the maple trees outside blew up like chiffon skirts and the earth roared. We huddled under the bedcovers and held tightly to Mom in the small, pine-paneled bedroom where my parents slept. We cringed at sounds hitting the roof and whined at every thunderclap. There was nothing to do but endure the crashing sounds around us, the spectacular lightning and the wet, clean smell of being in the midst of the earth's downpour. Sometimes the flashing strikes came very close and we wondered if anything would be left outside once it let up. I buried my head in a pillow that had a faint odor of mothballs, and cried softly.

I looked into my mother's eyes, wanting to find the familiar reassurances of my fierce protector. What I found instead was the hardness of her emerald pupils staring through me in terror. From that day on, I somehow I knew that I was alone and could only rely on myself.

The summer of the year my dad died brought back the acute pain of my aloneness once again. So when Mom asks me to spend Father's Day weekend with her, shortly after his death, I make plans to do so, and also schedule interviews about the book I have just completed.

I can set my watch by her routines. I know she will be home waiting for me when my taxi pulls up from the Newark Airport a little after seven in the evening, because it is Friday.

On Fridays at three o'clock she is with Mr. Oscar, the stylist down the street from Saks. The appointment takes precisely two hours, door to door. When she arrives home by five, her hair is a freshly revived color of strawberry blonde, teased up around her head like cotton candy. Her nails are polished with a fresh coat of bright red raspberry.

She peers out of the crack in the chained front door, unlocks the deadbolt and stands there with a big smile on her face.

Once inside the open door, I smell the familiar aroma of baked chicken and roasted potatoes coming from the oven. I know my mother has cooked one of my favorite meals.

She is wearing a brown-and-pink flowered muumuu that I sent her from Maui the year before. "I'm planning my trip to Maui with you for Thanksgiving. I think I will take this along. How do I look?" She lifts the hem of her skirt and makes a little twirl like she is on a modeling runway, then laughs.

Suddenly, she grabs me to her and hugs me. I smell the chicken on her apron. My stomach tightens. I am frightened of her intensity, but I want her attention and warmth, even when it inevitably turns cloying.

We wash up and sit down to eat dinner as soon as I put my bags down. "Well, aren't you going to say anything?" she asks.

"About what?" I answer innocently.

"About the car!"

"The car?"

"Did you see how it was parked in the driveway?" she asks with a big grin on her face.

"Oh, you learned how to back out and drive in straight. Congratulations," I say laughingly. "How does it feel to drive?"

"Well, it's very scary. I can get out of the driveway now, as long as I am careful not to run over the rose bushes parked alongside the Humbargs' house. But the drivers on the street are *meshugeh*. If they bother me, I let them have it with the horn."

I picture her honking her way through an intersection, blaring her way past gridlocked cars, even scaring off carjackers with her horn.

"What do you want to do this weekend?" she asks, as if we haven't discussed it many times before on the telephone.

"We could go to temple," I respond, knowing it is already too late to dress and drive to the eight o'clock Sabbath services. It is one of those non-conversations with my mother. If I don't say it, she will.

"No, by the time we get done eating, it will be too late." My mom shovels two more roasted potatoes onto my plate and talks quickly. "Do you want to go to temple tomorrow morning? Aren't you hungry? Did you eat on the plane? Didn't you know I would have dinner for you? Didn't you save room for my chicken? I thought you liked my chicken."

I feel my stomach tighten. "I *like* your chicken," I say. "No, I didn't eat on the plane." I have only been here six minutes and already I feel myself getting irritated. I know that not eating her overdone meal will be grounds for an argument about her cooking. In fact, thanks to my mom, I have developed a taste for overdone foods as long as there is a lot of ketchup, salt or gravy around.

"Only poor people eat pasta," Mom said when carbohydrates and grains became the trend. "In our house, we always made you kids eat steak and potatoes. So you would be healthy." I tried to sneak in fresh fruits and vegetables when we shopped for food together.

I look around the kitchen and try to calm myself down. The telephone conversations had shielded me. Now, face-to-face, it is different. I don't know what to expect. Will she suddenly turn angry and sour, or will she be my best girlfriend until I disagree with her about something? A small infraction can become a big blowup.

Nothing in the house has changed since Dad's funeral. My first attempts at oil painting from when I was in junior high are still hanging on the wall of the kitchen. The trees are the shapes of lollipops. When I was in college and brought dates home, I begged her to take down the pictures, but she insisted on keeping them up.

"I see you still have my painting," I joke with her, trying to change my mood and get the conversation back on track.

"At least I got to decorate our house with the art lessons we paid for."

So far, the conversation has stayed away from Dad. I want to talk about him, but can't find a gracious segue into the topic. So I finally launch into it clumsily. "Has Dad come to visit you yet? I mean, has he shown you a sign?" I ask my mom tentatively.

"No. Has he for you?"

"No," I say. There is a long pause then, she changes the subject.

I don't want to tell her about David and me making love to Dad's music because that was sex. Mom and I never broach sex in any form.

"Did I tell you that they are filming a cookie commercial on our street? Our house might be right in the commercial, along with Mrs. Nottinghams's and Mrs. Lynn's," Mom says.

"Why this street?" I ask.

"It's Keebler's. They want an old-fashioned 1930's-type neighborhood. We were chosen. The Nottingham and Lynn people are getting about five hundred dollars for the shot. I don't know about me. I should tell them that I'm charging them for their using our sidewalk."

It feels odd discussing this or anything but Dad's absence, but I can't bring that up and neither can she. This hesitancy seems odd in light of what we've been through. "Can I sleep with you tonight like we did when Dad was in the hospital?" I ask when we are getting ready to go upstairs.

I need to hold her and be close to her. I'm not sure how she will react. I feel fragile and I don't want to be rejected. It is getting dark and I am feeling alone. "When I slept with you last time, you felt soft and cuddly, like a croissant. David feels hard like a Kaiser roll." I try to ease the moment into humor.

"Soft and greasy," she teases.

I awake briefly in the middle of the night. Her back is towards me as she sleeps. In that moment, I feel desperate to say all the things that I have never said to her, but I have no words inside me, only feelings. I long to make all the crazy rebellious and bad things I did to hurt them right again. I want my dad back so badly that I ache.

But there is something different about her. Of course, it's obvious that she is grieving the loss of Dad. She is quieter and more subdued than usual, but there is something else. I can feel it tonight as we hold each other, sleeping spoon-style. There is a disturbing quality of no one home in her body as she sleeps, as if she is visiting somewhere else and will return in the morning.

I awake alone. I smell freshly brewing coffee and hear the click of the silverware as Mom places it in the dishwasher. She must have been up for hours, I think sleepily.

When I come downstairs. Mom is sitting at the kitchen table, fully dressed and reading my manuscript. She looks up from the book. "You know, I can really read this! It's really interesting! And look at the dedication to Saul and Sarah! This is a *beshert* (gift)!" she exclaims.

That word *beshert* resonates deep inside me. Yet I ask reflexively, "What do you mean, you can really read it?"

"Well, I thought it would be more academic and not something I would understand. But I do. I can relate to people losing their jobs," she says. "I remember Dad losing his job and going through the things you describe." She puts down the manuscript. "When do I get my own copy, autographed by the author?" she asks, smiling.

I can feel something deep inside my chest open and relax after so long. I finally feel validated by my mother. "When it gets published in October," I say. "Meanwhile, could you help me practice the answers to this interview coming up? Could you quiz me?" I hand her three sheets with questions and answers I have prepared that a reporter might ask.

Mom looks it over, asks a few questions and hands it back to me. "Dear, if you wrote the book, you know the answers."

"It just helps keep me from being nervous if I'm well prepared," I answer.

"You've always been like that. Just stop it, and let's go," she says.

I change the subject because I feel like I am getting too close to talking about how fragile I feel about going to New York, doing this interview with a reporter from *The Wall Street Journal* and meeting my publisher. "So, is the new driver going to drive this morning?" I ask.

"Well, actually, I'd rather let you drive. I think I need more practice," she says.

Inwardly, I breathe a sigh of relief. I can't get used to all these changes. A father who is dead. A mother who drives a car.

"But, let me tell you! Rhonda and I are planning a trip in August to go drive to Pittsburgh and visit Mildred and Herman. We will take turns driving," she says smiling.

"Oh, a kind of Thelma and Louise trip." I can see that this just cracks her up. She is such a great audience sometimes.

"Yes, a Thelma and Louise trip. Rhonda is Thelma and I am Louise, I guess." She gives a hearty chuckle. "Now which is which? I forget. Drink your coffee and let's go! We'll go to the cleaners first, then to temple. Then let's have lunch at Don's Drive-In. I've just got to run upstairs to the attic and see if I remembered to get some wool skirts back from the cleaners. My memory isn't what it used to be."

I traipse after her up two flights of carpeted stairs to a room with bare planks on the floor and a roof with rafters. If the basement is cool and damp and belongs to my dad and Harry, the attic is hot and dry and belongs to my mother. There are boxes of clothes, linens and shoes, and a big metal cabinet that houses her winter clothes, meticulously ordered in the center of the attic. The rest of the attic recedes into dark corners and crawl space.

"I've thrown out a lot of stuff, so when I go, you won't have to drag all of my belongings to the curb outside, the way the Hamilton kids did. It was awful to see Mrs. Hamilton's most intimate possessions set on the curb. Anyone could come by and pick through them. Like animals, it was," she says.

15

When we lined up in gym in our pale blue shirts and puffy navy cotton bloomers, Beverly, the tallest, was always at the front of the line. I was at the end — the shortest girl in our class. She lorded this over me, but this day she seemed in a friendlier mood.

That morning Mom had loaned me her new umbrella. It trailed behind me, making a rat-tat-tat sound on the sidewalk.

Beverly attended the Catholic Church on the corner. She drank wine and ate crackers there, and knelt to pray to the Virgin Mary. Her God looked like a woman holding a dead man in her arms. The Virgin had long dark hair, blue and white flowing robes, and a sad, downcast face.

What did the face of my God look like? I wondered as I walked. If I met him on the street, for instance, would he be wearing business clothes like my dad, or a sport shirt and baseball cap like coach Hoffmeyer? I turned and asked Beverly, "What does God look like?"

Suddenly, she grabbed my hat and ran up the hill with it, laughing and shouting to Joan, who was behind me. I took off after her, but soon I was in the middle of the two girls, who were tossing my hat back and forth over my head.

"Shorty! Jew girl! Jew girl!" taunted Joan. The sky grew threatening.

Something inside me snapped. I had had enough. I rushed at Joan like a seventy-pound pit bull and pushed her into the hedges. As the sky grew darker, I lifted my umbrella and aimed at her head — reckless and wildly swinging. Months of humiliation, rejection and frustration rushed up from my belly and out through my arms.

She crouched, hiding her head in her hands, as I relentlessly struck her harder, again and again. Suddenly, the umbrella cracked under the stress, and a large piece of it flew into her eye before it landed on the other side of the hedge.

I saw tears and blood gush from her face. She lay crumpled on the ground. Beverly had run away. "That'll teach you to call me names!" I shrieked, shocked by what I had done. I ran home.

"What happened to my umbrella?" Mom snapped. What was left of the umbrella was in her hand.

"I broke it." Uncontrollable tears streamed down my face. This was the final straw. I felt hopeless and alone. Rain and hail finally came at that moment, hitting the window with chunks of ice.

"That was my new umbrella!" she screamed. "What did you do to it?" Mom moved toward me menacingly.

"It was Joan. She called me 'Jew Girl' and 'Shorty,' so I hit her over the head with it."

Mom looked at me closely. I could see anger and fear in her face. "Did you hurt her?"

I froze. "Yes, I think so. I left her in the bushes."

"*Mazel tov*. She had it coming. Good you should do that. She deserved it. Don't worry about the umbrella, I'll buy a new one on Saturday, so next time you can do it harder. Maybe that will help her mouth!"

She laughed and hugged me. I let myself laugh, but it really was a laugh of relief. I was disarmed by Mom's sudden support for me. She had never done that before.

That Saturday, Mom and I took a bus into Newark. We looked at many umbrellas, but then she saw a red raincoat with a matching umbrella. "Why, this is just made for you." She picked it off the hanger. Red was my favorite color.

"When my brother and I were growing up, my mother worked hard at the delicatessen, so I had to take care of him. We were close, maybe because he was a sickly kid." Mom was sitting in a little chair in the fitting room, looking up at me as I turned slowly around admiring my coat in the mirror. The room was small and the air was stale, but in this moment I felt an intimacy I rarely felt with her. In telling me this story, she was taking me in her confidence.

"I had to fight his battles because all the other kids picked on him. They called him names like 'Jew boy.' But I really whipped those kids. They knew they had to deal with me if they messed with him."

"What do you think of this raincoat?" I asked her, starting to feel slightly uncomfortable with her expectations of me.

She glanced at it and continued, "You can't let Beverly know that she hurt you, or she will try again and again."

"But she *did* hurt my feelings," I said.

"Feelings, schmeelings! You mustn't let it show. Act as if nothing happened. It will get her goat."

I was still standing staring in the mirror at myself, quite certain that my mother surely didn't understand what was going on.

"Red is your color." She leaned forward, poked her head

out of the fitting room and waved to the passing sales girl. "We'll take it!"

"Doesn't show the blood!" Harry said, when I modeled my purchase at home in front of him.

But the raincoat and the new umbrella didn't stop Beverly from beating me up again. And my mother realized that she couldn't protect me, even in absentia, like she had done for her brother.

In seventh grade, I was one of the last ones in my class to get my period. When I finally did, I nagged mom to get me a bra, but she decided to save an extra trip and get me a girdle as well. To celebrate this new me, Mom took me down to Klein's Ladies Foundation department. The counters were high and the lighting was bright.

That day, Mom decided to get a new girdle as well. My mother's naked body in the fitting room made me think of something that could be easily hurt, like a turtle without a shell. Her underwear was like armor: the bra cups were rocket cones and the hose stayed shaped like someone else's legs when you took them off. Mom wiggled out of her long-line girdle, which immediately shrank up with a dull snapping noise at her ankles.

She hated girdles. The first thing she said when she came home from work was, "Don't talk to me until I take my girdle off," or "Let me get out of this girdle before we talk." as if her ability to articulate was being strangled by several feet of latex. In the summer, it left a diamond-shaped control panel imprint on her belly. Most of the girdle was latex, but the diamond — shaped like an icon of something sacred guarding her womb — was always satin.

"The big hippo and the little hippo," Harry quipped when he saw Mom's large latex girdle hanging alongside my minuscule one on the shower curtain after they were washed.

The Ladies Foundation department was certainly my rite of passage that day. A hugely endowed saleslady with a tape measure around her neck greeted my mother and ushered us into one of the largest fitting rooms I had ever seen. It was my first three-way mirror, and the first time that I ever stood in front of one on a little platform.

The matronly lady took the tape measure off her neck and gently shimmied it around my bodice, like a skilled surgeon. I was a grand thirty inches in the bust. My hips measured thirty-four. I saw a glance shoot from the saleslady to my mother and back.

I felt defeated. It was like putting a rubber band around a stick.

The saleslady left the fitting room and came back with a hand full of items that looked like little poached eggs on straps. These were padded bras — the 1950's version of the Miracle Bra.

"We just got in a new line of undergarments for the slimline figure," she proudly announced.

"A size 30 B fits her nicely," Mom said, after some tugging and pulling around my breasts. I hated how close and intimate she was now. In that moment I was so sorry we came, and how we all were making such a big deal about these breasts of mine. How these spongy rocket cups jammed on top and pulled snug. I could hardly breathe, so I pulled my shoulders up.

"Stop that!" my mother snapped.

While the saleslady left to get some girdles, Mom sat down and looked at me with a critical eye. "Now you mustn't let any boy pet with you. You must save yourself until your wedding night. Boys talk, and if they find out that you are easy, they won't want to marry you."

I was filled with shame and embarrassment as I stood almost buck-naked in front of my mother. I didn't understand how Dad could be the Prince Charming on one hand, but you had to be on your guard with men on the other.

I had already sat in the back rows of the movie theater for the Saturday afternoon matinee with boys trying to grope me. I couldn't share that with her.

At school, everyone knew about how Vivian Epman had necked with Buddy Vernet. When he reached in to touch the real "gold," instead, he got a green skein of wool that she had wadded up there. Kids called her 'green wool' for several years. I couldn't even look Vivian in the face after that. If that happened to me I would kill myself.

There was so much to know, and at that moment I felt a competition with my mom around men in general. I wanted her to tell me the truth, but I knew deep down inside that she wasn't the most up–to-date about these things, and she already did not approve of the way my life seemed to be headed. But in 1957, there seemed to be no other direction available to me. She didn't have the information that I wanted. In her mind, it was still the 1930's world of red lipstick, big-shouldered dresses and saving yourself until you got married.

16

Mom waits in the car when I stop by my cousin Denny's dry cleaning store to retrieve some of her winter skirts.

In third grade, Denny was my only friend. I saw him every Saturday afternoon when my dad visited his sister Clara and my Grandma at their two-story walk-up in Newark. Denny and I would go off and play Old Maid, Pick Up Sticks, Candy Land or Checkers. Aunt Helen said that we were "thick as thieves," and we were. Denny was a sweet and kind kid, and it never mattered that he was a year younger than I was.

He had big brown eyes and an easy laugh. My mother would pat his thick brown hair and say he had bedroom eyes, and my aunt would chuckle at that. Uncle Moe joined in by saying that Denny was going to be a lady-killer.

I didn't know what a lady-killer was, but I took it for granted that Denny was going to be a rock star when he grew up, although I had no such grand plans for myself. This was the 1950's and I, like other girls my age, knew we would work only long enough to find the right man, settle down and have kids. Every verbal and visual message I'd grown up with telegraphed that a girl child belonged with someone else, a male partner, signaling the world that she was going about the business of being a helpful and charming female, bent on caring for the needs of others — a nurse, a teacher or a librarian. But *I knew* that Denny was destined for something great.

He thought so, too. Sometimes, when we made forts under his covers on the bed he shared with his older brother Stevie, he would tell me his grand plans. So it came as a surprise, many years later, when I returned from the Peace Corps to find out that he was running a dry cleaning business on the corner of Springfield and Millburn Avenues in Short Hills, New Jersey.

I walk into the store with a receipt for Mom's woolen skirts and wait in line. Finally, a black woman behind the counter looks up and says in a flat tone, "How may I help you?"

I hand her the slip my mom has given me, and wait while she spins the big automated rack behind her to find the order. Past the counter, I see a vast room filled with rack of clothes in plastic and black people sorting, pressing, sewing and carrying racks out back to opened doors, where trucks wait on the other side of the building.

Someone barely resembling my cousin comes out of a windowless office to the side. He is medium height, dense and compact. He swaggers as he walks. He wears chinos, a plaid shirt made of shiny material and several gold chains around his neck. His hair is thinning on top and he sports long side-burns. He resembles an aging Elvis Presley — potbelly and tinted aviator glasses.

Just as I am about to greet him, two heavy-set men in brown suits push past me and shout to him, "We're lookin' for a Garcia Rodriquez. You got him employed here?" They both pull out badges as I watch from several yards to the side.

Denny focuses his attention through his bifocals on the two men. "He ain't working here today. He called in sick. Why, any trouble?"

"Yeah, he's wanted for assault and battery on his wife. We gotta bring him in."

Denny shrugs, a what-can-I-do shrug, takes both detectives by the arm and ushers them out to the sidewalk. I walk closer toward the open door to hear what he is saying. After all his dreams, he struggles with illegal aliens and dry cleaning. "I don't want any trouble here. My clientele don't have to hear this," he says. "Give me your cards and I will call the minute he comes to work."

The detectives hand him their cards and leave in their unmarked car.

Meanwhile, I pay for Mom's skirts and thank the woman behind the counter. She walks to the back and starts talking in soft tones to the men putting garments in canvas baskets.

As Denny steps back in the door, I greet him. "Hey, are you back here to see your mom? Sorry to hear about you dad." He shakes my hand like a politician. I look into his guarded brown eyes and see a wariness that is defending him against anything soft, emotional or raw. This is a different Denny from the one I knew as a kid.

In that moment, I want desperately to talk to that sweet, innocent little boy I played with. I don't want to be inappropriate, so I say instead, "I picked up some stuff for Mom, she's waiting for me. *How are you*?"

I elongate each word, trying to get to something real inside him. I can't say, hey, Denny remember the time we played Candy Land under your bed, so our brothers couldn't find us? Remember how your brother showed us how to diddle your puppy? Or our first sex lesson? Then we could laugh together, and it would feel like all these years didn't count. But something in his eyes tells me that he won't approve of my bringing up those innocent times forty-seven years later. Those times are gone.

"Denny, you still playing drums in a band?" I ask brazenly. "Remember your plans to be famous?" I can't believe what I am saying.

I see his face redden with embarrassment. "That was bullshit. I'm okay," he says, taking my arm and nodding to a few customers while ushering me outside. Once on the street, he stands with feet planted firmly on the cement, hands in his pockets and his attention riveted somewhere in the middle of my face. With his tinted glasses, it is hard to tell what he's focusing on.

"Life is strange," he begins. "You saw those two guys? That trouble happens here almost every week. I work my ass off and what do I get? More trouble with immigration, employment services and the police. For what? Just to feed my family. They think money grows on trees. Ya know, my three boys are all applying to college and one may go to medical school. My youngest girl, Penny, is in high school now. Time flies. How's your husband?"

Denny seems uncomfortable. I have caught him in the middle of an awkward situation. "Fine. He's back in California," I say.

"Yeah, California. Life is good there. Well, this here ain't California. I see *Bay Watch* and *Entertainment Tonight*. But I got this boat, see, and when things get too bad, I just disappear. I mean, the wife knows where to find me and everything, but I mean I just go!" He shoots his hand up in the air to signify freedom.

I hate how he seems to have to justify his life to me. It is as if he is comparing himself to some fantasy he has about me because I live in California. Does he think everyone has a lifestyle like *Bay Watch*?

"Your mom gonna sell the house now?" he asks.

Maybe I have created too much of an opening. I recoil. My dad hasn't been gone very long, and besides, I haven't seen

Denny in over forty years. I find myself in the middle of a strange conversation with a man whom I know from childhood. Out of politeness, I just keep going.

"No, she wants to keep living there," I say.

Denny steps back and raises his index finger and begins pontificating, and I can't stop him. "You are going to leave your mom, like a dog, to live alone in that house? Even a dog has companionship!"

I begin to feel small and childish. He starts to shout right there on Millburn Street, but passersby don't pay much attention. "Even a dog has a bowl with food and water. Even a dog has company. How can you do that to her? She should move to Florida like my mom, and sell her house. That house is too big for her."

"Denny, I told you, she doesn't want to. She told me!" I see this conversation is going nowhere, but I am caught in the middle of a crazy dialogue I can't get out of, and now I start to feel angry and agitated.

He shouts, "She doesn't know what she needs. You just tell her, that's all," he shouts.

"I should tell her?" I find myself lapsing into some other person, a cross between Bella Abzug and a Jewish fishmonger. I am becoming someone I hardly know, bullied and patronized by the person Denny has become.

"I should tell her?" I repeat. "I don't see you telling your mother anything! Does your mother ever listen to you? No, she is as crazy and opinionated as they come. It's no secret that everyone in our family breathed easy once she left for Florida." I am clearly out of control, but I am not going to walk away feeling beaten and demeaned. I stop short.

Denny steps back. His face is red. "I just think an old woman like your mother shouldn't live alone. It's your job to talk some sense into her."

"Denny," I say, "my mother has more common sense in her whole body than your mother has in her...." Before I can finish, a black lady from the store comes rushing out, shouting. "Mr. Franch, Mr. Franch, come quick! Garcia just walked into the store."

Denny blushes. He starts walking quickly backwards and says, "I gotta go. Great to see ya. Say hi to your mom for me."

I walk slowly to the car feeling shamed and abused. I long for that sweet boy to share my hurt and sorrow with about my dad's death, but what I have found is a stranger. I want so badly to feel softness between us and a recognition of our old tender times together.

It comes as no surprise, several hours later, when my mom asks me why Denny's wife called and complained that I had been nasty to Denny and said some awful things about his mother. Everyone in our family knew that my Aunt Helen was "off her rocker." Even Mom laughed about it. But my exchange with Denny is just one more of those things that I don't know how to explain to my mom.

By the time we get to temple B'nai Shoffar, the sun is high in the sky. "It's going to be another scorcher," Mom says.

I hate these hot, humid days when my hair gets frizzy. I can already feel the sweat forming on the inside of my blouse. There are so many vacant spaces in the parking lot of the temple that I am able to park right in front.

"Most people are away on vacation," Mom says.

The big granite walls create a dark, cool feeling inside. This is probably one of the few places in New Jersey with no air conditioning. The temple is sparsely filled with people in their seventies and eighties. The men are in shirtsleeves and the women in cool-looking summer frocks. Seats are roped off in the back to force members to sit in the forward section.

My mother and I stand by the wall, away from the people finding seats. I keep hoping that I will find a familiar face, someone with whom I went to school with, so that I'll feel like I belong here. But I never really felt like I belonged here, even when I was a kid. This place was for rich kids and their parents. My parents always seemed too inhibited, too withdrawn to allow themselves to be included. They went home and criticized what they saw. I only felt an ancient, indescribable ache. Perhaps I have imagined that if we went here, I would feel secure. But I don't — just another thing I can't tell my mother.

"Why would you feel strange here? This is your temple. We joined so that you and Harry would have something," she would say.

She leads me over to the foyer and shows me a plaque, among several hundred other plaques, that has the Perlman name on it. "Just wanted to show you that we are also one of the muckity-mucks at this temple. Dad and I also have a perpetual *Yahrtzeit*," she adds.

"What do you mean?"

"When I die, we are all paid up, so the rabbi can't come and ask you for more money to say the blessing over us on the anniversary of our death," she says. "We had it all taken care of so we wouldn't be a burden to you and Harry."

We file out silently after the service into the glaring sun, and drive to Don's Drive-In. As we turn into the parking lot, Mom says, "This place has certainly changed since you were in high school. It got really upscale. Even their prices are more expensive. You and Harvey Hochman used to come here after the movies."

"Yeah, remember the time when he was learning how to fly, and made me take a double sheet and spread it out in the street in front of our house so he could recognize our place, and buzz it?"

172

"He was a crazy guy!" Mom says laughingly. "Yeah, you were sitting in the living room, kissing. I came in and asked what you both were doing. I mean I knew you were kissing, but I didn't want that in my house. So he said to me, 'We are French kissing, Mrs. Perlman,' I said, 'What's that?' So he took me in his arms and kissed me! Well, Dad, who was sitting in the den, saw this and shouted, 'Sarah, you come here right now!' I was shocked."

"All I remember is that you and Dad were really wound up in your underwear about him." Dad once went out of the house to get some newspapers. He hopped into his car in the driveway, didn't see that Harvey had parked his little M.G. behind Dad's big Cutlass, and plowed right into it. It was something out of *All in the Family* where Dad was so exasperated by Harvey he just unconsciously plowed right into him. I remind Mom of the event.

"What made it so embarrassing was that he had to call his insurance guy and tell him what happened. It was all Dad's fault. And Dad hated to be wrong."

After lunch, we drive into Bloomfield center to get Mom the right orthopedic shoes. I sit in the cool, air-conditioned store, watching Mom try on pair after pair of white sandals.

"Why don't you buy a pair like this? They're so comfortable," she asks me as she waits for the salesman

"Nah."

I have it in my mind to get a pair like hers, but suddenly change my mind. I am scared that part of me is turning into her.

Before I went downstairs that morning, I had tried on her nightgown. It was lying on the other side of the bed. To my surprise, it fit. I had never fit into my mother's clothes before. I was becoming her, I thought when I saw myself in the mirror with her nightgown on. I looked like a younger version of my mother. I was confused. I never really liked her, and now I was looking like her. I mean, I would have never chosen her for my mother.

"I can wear these when we go to New York on Monday to visit your publisher," she announces.

"My agent thought it was odd to take my mother with me, but then she changed her mind and began to think it was very interesting," I say. And as a way of passing time I add, "Have you decided what you're going to wear?"

"Well, if we have to walk a lot, I can wear my old white sandals like this, and my white linen sheath with gold buttons. It's hanging on the door to Harry's room. When we get to the interview, I can switch to my little open-toe heels. Would that work?"

"Sure, that sounds fine." I am thinking about how one minute I can't get far enough away from her and the next, I have her accompanying me to the most important meeting in my life, with the publisher of my new book. That's the way it is when I stay more than one night. I begin feeling like her, even having impulses to buy the same old-lady shoes. Yet, more and more recently, I don't mind that feeling as much. Several years ago, I would have taken rat poison rather than feel good about buying her old-lady shoes.

17

Driving home that afternoon, watching the heat rise off the tarmac streets, I decide that what I need is some separation from my mom's incessant chatter and company. I go up to the Hilton and work out, using my Nautilus club card.

When I return an hour and a half later, Mom hasn't unbolted the back door like she usually does. I unlock the door and go in.

"I'm up here." I follow her voice and find her in bed. Something seems wrong. "I feel nauseous, and I have these shooting pains in my back. It's probably something I ate at the deli. I shouldn't have eaten the mayo," she says quietly.

"Is there something I can get you?"

She looks pale and tired. I am certain she will pull herself up off the bed any minute and go downstairs to make supper. I have never seen her lying in bed in the middle of the day. Sometimes she would say, after she pushed her chair back from the dinner table, "You know what I'm going to do right after I clean up the kitchen?" And without waiting for an answer, she'd say, "I'm going to go upstairs and lie down and get my strength back."

That was what she always said she was going to do, and she always announced it as if it were an idea that had just occurred to her, a hopeful decision. But she never did actually go upstairs and lie down. By the end of the dishes, she would be on the phone, or in the den watching television while crocheting a shawl, or talking to my dad above the blare of the television.

"I took two Advil just before you came home."

The half-full water glass is on the night table.

"How was your workout?" she asks politely.

"It was okay," I say. She lays her head back on the pillow and closes her eyes.

Several hours go by, and she sleeps on and off.

The heat of the day seeps into the bedroom. The ancient air conditioner makes occasional gurgling and sighing sounds as it drones on. I sit at her side, read or doze off too. Later, I wake with a start. My mom is lying next to me, looking at me through half-closed eyes.

"How do you feel now?" I ask softly.

"Not good," she says.

I ask hesitatingly, "Should I call 911?"

"No!" she snaps. "Let's wait. Maybe it will go away."

"But Mom, it's Saturday night! If we wait too long, the emergency room will be crowded."

I glance at the clock on Dad's dresser, noting that nothing in the room had been removed since Dad died. Even his laundry bag of dirty clothes still hangs on the inside of the doorknob.

Mom dozes off again. I grow hungry, so I go downstairs to see if I can find something to eat. As I pass through the living room, I feel a menacing presence. The portrait of my dad hanging above the mantel seems formidable and angry. It is dim in the kitchen. I open the refrigerator and find some leftover brisket. I make myself a sandwich by the light of the open refrigerator door.

When I return upstairs, Mom is awake and says, "Did you warm up the brisket and potatoes? I was going to make that tonight for supper."

"It is just fine cold. Do you want me to warm some up for you? I left you sleeping, so I wasn't sure."

Mom winces suddenly.

"Don't you think we should get help?" I ask her. "This isn't going away." I look at the clock. It occurs to me that she has been in pain since I came back at five, and now it is eight. "I guess the Advil has worn off." She winces again.

"Oh God! Oh God!" she cries suddenly.

I feel like a little girl, wanting my mother to tell me what to do. She always tells me what to do. "Mom, I want to call 911 before it gets too late, and you get the emergency room filled with Saturday night drunks with knife wounds."

Mom looks at me and I see fear shoot through her eyes. I grab her bedside rotary phone. I am sobbing and dialing 911. "Honey, don't go to pieces on me now," she manages to say.

"Oh, Mom, I'm not going to pieces. I'm just crying."

"Well, I need you now," she says softly.

Within seconds, I hear the approaching whine of an ambulance siren break the stillness of the oppressive, humid evening. As it nears the house, only the red lights silently flash, making moving shadows across the dark neighborhood houses, but in my head I still hear the high-pitched siren as I run downstairs to open the door.

"Take my purse to the hospital and lock the doors," my mother orders as she is lifted and carried down the stairway by two densely built men in white uniforms. I follow behind her, hearing old dialogues of my mother's voice in my head. *Now, watch the wallpaper! I just had the house redone and it cost a pretty penny. Don't let these men linger and take a look around, or something may be missing when you come home*. I want to do everything right, just like she wants. No mistakes. They lift her into the van, while small clusters of neighbors I don't recognize gather at a generous distance across the street.

My mom is okay, I tell myself. She will be better tomorrow morning. This is unneeded. Why did I call? She is never sick. I shouldn't have done this. This sacred space, intruded and shattered by strangers. Only Jews enter this house, this fortress, this birdcage of a castle. What have I done?

The ambulance speeds off down the street with my mother, leaving me dumbfounded and standing alone on the street. I look back at the house. All the lights are on upstairs and the front door is wide open. Bugs swarm around the porch lights. The neighbors huddle and watch, mute.

"If you need a ride, I can drive you up there." Kathy Humbarg, the next-door neighbor, steps forward.

I am jarred back into the moment by her voice. "Yes. I could use the company. But I'll drive."

Following the signs to the hospital, we easily arrive at the emergency room. In one of the partitioned rooms, I find my mother stretched out on a gurney. Kathy waits for me outside in reception. Mom is dozing when I rush in. "How are you?" I ask.

"I'm okay. They took some tests. Talk to the doctor." She closes her eyes.

I run into the corridor and bump into a tall young man with black hair. He wears a plastic name tag that says, "Dr. Monte."

"Are you Mrs. Perlman's daughter?" he asks.

"Yes. How is she?" I ask.

"We did some tests. They show up okay. All her functions — liver, heart, kidney — seem okay. What was she complaining of?"

"She has a pain in her back and arm that won't go away," I say.

"We'll keep here overnight for observation, do more tests and contact her doctor. She may need surgery, if it's what I think it is. Gall bladder," he adds.

I go back and tell my mother that her tests are good. She is tired, but seems pleased at the news. "Go home and get some rest," she says.

"I can't let you lie here by yourself. I'll stay."

In the early morning, Kathy gets a ride back with some neighbors, and an orderly comes in. "We'll be moving your mother up to a hospital bed," he tells me. "You'll need to leave." Mom is asleep, so I tiptoe out softly.

I open the door to the house at four a.m. and slowly walk in.

Suddenly, I feel my dad's presence. It is a growling and roaming energy. It rumbles past me. I go upstairs, quickly undress and get into bed. Before I turn off the light, I dial David's telephone number. I am in terror, so I push in the lock on the bedroom doorknob. It is about one in the morning on the West Coast, and David picks up on the first ring.

He answers in a sleepy voice, almost inaudible at first. "Hello." Just then it hits me. I begin to sob. I feel safe for the first time since I dialed 911 the night before.

"I took Mom to the emergency room tonight. They are giving her some tests and she is staying over. My dad is trying to take her. I can feel it. I can feel him roaming around the house looking for her. I just know it." I was crying hysterically.

"What?"

I can tell that he is trying to wake up, take all this in and respond reassuringly at the same time. As he listens to my retelling the events of the previous evening and early morning, he is stunned into silence.

"I know she is going to die. You just can't imagine what it feels like here."

"That's not going to happen. They won't do surgery on an eighty-year-old lady, so he can't take her, because they won't open her up."

He always knows the right thing to say. I feel relieved. Of course, I think, she will only die if they put her under and cut into her. By the time I hang up, I hear the newspaper truck starting and stopping along on the street. I turn off the drone of the air conditioning and draw open the shades a little. It is still dark outside.

I still feel my dad roaming around downstairs, and I don't want him to come into the bedroom looking for Mom, so I put a chair against the locked door. He is furious and restless.

"Tell me that Mom will be okay. Tell me she won't die," I pray. Only silence answers me. But David's words stay with me, and comfort me. If they don't open her up, if they don't operate on her, she will not die like Dad. She will come home at the end of the weekend. She will remain the strong, opinionated, healthy woman that I both love and hate. We will go on together in a new way.

Then I sleep. Hours later, the phone wakes me. It is the nurse at the hospital.

"We have your mother under observation. She's on Demerol and sedatives, and she's sleeping soundly."

I rush back to the hospital and sit at my mother's bedside. She dozes on and off all day. Occasionally she awakes, smiles at me and presses my hand. At about four o'clock in the afternoon, she opens her eyes and says, "Oh Honey, I'm sorry we're spending Father's Day this way."

I can't believe the irony of this whole thing. When Dad was alive, Father's Day was ushered in by searching for the perfect gift and showing him my love with a homemade card — something funny that exaggerated his foibles. Last night felt like a Stephen King movie plot. Now, in the bright afternoon light, I don't trust what I saw and felt.

"Don't worry, Mom." I sit back in the chair next to her bed. I feel really good being there quietly with her and watching her sleep. This woman is so self-reliant, but I am needed now. I like the reassuring feeling of sitting next to her and listening to her in-breath, a pause, and then her out-breath.

I am awaiting Dr. Arnstein's call. They did more tests on her. Maybe it is a hernia, an ulcer, or stress. I try to reach my brother and his wife who are vacationing in Oceanside, California, but the number Roberta gave me is wrong. She must have transposed the digits, I think. I sit by Mom's side and try to gain strength from her quiet breathing. So many Sunday afternoons spent together over a lifetime, but none like this one.

Again that night, I can't sleep. I hear low, rumbling thunderstorms outside, and Dad roaming around downstairs, searching for Mom. Finally, I take a sleeping pill. I dream that Dad comes to me and demands Mom. "You can take her. Just don't let her suffer," I tell him, confident that if they don't operate on her, open her up, she will be spared. Then the ghost of my Dad will be powerless.

In the morning, just before I am leaving for the city for an interview with *The Wall Street Journal,* I call Dr. Arnstein. "We can't find anything wrong with your mom, so she'll be released tomorrow. Don't worry. She's probably just exhausted from the last eight months of watching your dad die." I hang up, feeling relieved and free to spend the day in the Big City.

I go by limo to Manhattan. As we make our way through the back streets of Secaucus to avoid the morning traffic, I see a little red brick shack that sits in the middle of the swamp of Secaucus. It has been there since I was a child. I remember trips in the car with Mom and Dad. We had a joke about that shack. I'd say, "Dad, what is that house out there in the middle of the swamp?" And he would respond, "It's the poor house, where you and your mother are sending me." It would send my brother and me into fits of laughter.

My publisher barely has time for me, since he is already birthing his next book. His publicist and my publicist hit it off well. My publicist, Paul, is young, eager to do well and enthusiastic. He has only been at the public relations agency for two months and was trained as a dancer. I think that he'll need to do a lot of fancy footwork on this job.

This reality feels tangible. I feel that I am moving my life and the commerce of it along — palpable and thick with possibilities. The last two nights feel far away. Occasionally, I feel a surge of joy knowing that Mom is going to be released from the hospital in twenty-four hours.

As I make my way through the day, I realize that taking my mother along would have been a mistake. She would have been upset by the crush of the lunchtime crowds, the torpor, the dirt, the size of the building. The noise level alone is deafening. We get lost, and I break the heel of my shoe. I am hot and sweaty even in my summer silk. I give an interview in *The Wall Street Journal* cafeteria over the din of plates and lunchtime chatter, because the journalist works out of a noisy cubicle. I find her style of interviewing tactless and attacking, but I am on top of it. Mom is right. I know my stuff — after all, I wrote the book. Still, I feel caught between wishing for fame — the Wayne Dyer style of doing it — and the reality of my dead dad, and Mom in the hospital. The uncertainty of it all and the magnitude of what I am juggling that day is almost too much. I am happy to be interviewed and to be doing well, but part of me wants to be sitting next to Mom's bedside listening to her breathe.

It is only later that night, after I check in with Mom in the hospital, report the events of the day to her, and check my phone messages to see if my brother has called, that I can feel

Dad's presence again in the silence of the house. He is calm. He is not roaming. All I can hear is the ticking of the clock on the mantel below his portrait. Whatever craziness I have endured in my imagination the previous evenings is gone. I get my first good night's sleep in days.

I awake early the next morning, and organize Mom's clothes in a bag to bring to the hospital so that she won't have to wear her bathrobe and slippers home. The week's heat breaks and the day is cooler. I make coffee downstairs and joyfully leave the house at seven a.m., knowing that today is the day Mom is going to come home. I'll be on a plane back to California by noon. Maybe after this scare, Mom will be more open to moving to Mill Valley and living in a cute little house that we'll buy for her, or maybe even live with us.

The guard recognizes me and waves me through the hospital gate near the emergency entrance. I run up to Mom's room just as she is finishing her breakfast. I have to leave by nine to catch the cab back at home by ten-thirty, and then I'll go to the airport.

She sits up in bed when she sees me. "I feel drugged. I feel very spun up and anxious this morning," she says but then she sees the bag. "What did you bring for me?" She seems like her old, feisty self as she motions toward the shopping bag I carry.

"I brought you the Hawaiian dress. I thought that you might like to wear it home," I say.

"You have such a sweet heart," she says softly, and reaches up to touch my cheek. I put the bag down on the chair just as the nurse comes in.

"When was the last time you gave me Demerol?" asks my mother.

"Three a.m. That was the regular medication time, just like the doctor prescribed," responds the nurse.

Mom lays her head back on the pillow.

"I still have that pain," she says, pointing to her back. Just at that moment, a black woman comes in, pushing a wheelchair.

"Are you Mrs. Perlman?" She doesn't wait for a response. "I have orders here for you to be transported to the x-ray downstairs."

"I can walk."

The gaunt woman says, "Look, I am just the transporter. I'm supposed to wheel you there." She waves a paper in the air, presumably the orders from Dr. Arnstein.

The woman helps mom into the wheelchair. There is something strange about her that I can't put my finger on. Maybe it is how still she stands in her tall, aging body, or her lack of friendliness.

Mom turns to me and says, "Let's say goodbye here, or you'll miss your plane."

My stomach lurches. "No, I have time. I made time," I insist.

The three of us board the empty elevator. Through the window across from the elevator door, I catch a glimpse of the sun rising in the morning sky. It is going to be a scorcher.

The transporter, Mom and I maintain an uncomfortable silence during the ride, until I ask her, "How long have you worked at the hospital?"

"Oh, quite awhile," she says evasively. I just get a bad feeling about this woman. I feel a return of the same menacing energy from several nights before.

When we get to the x-ray department, Mom insists again that I leave. I feel uncomfortable turning her over to this woman. "No. I want to stay here with you until you are done. I have time," I tell her.

We sit in the reception area silently until a young woman calls her into the room with the metal x-ray table and large machines that hang from the ceiling.

I go into the bathroom and close the door to the corridor. This bathroom has another door that opens into the x-ray room. I go to shut it.

Through it, I catch a glimpse of the back of my mother in a patient gown, and I hear a low moan and some muttering. "I'm in pain! I'm in pain!" she groans.

I quickly open the door and stand there. I hear her groan again. This time, the technician sounds an alarm, and from everywhere in that department people come running. "Code blue! Code blue!" says a voice in an even tone on the loudspeaker overhead.

Someone shoves me out of the room and slams the door in my face. I stand dumbfounded. My legs feel weak under me. I lean against a cart full of freshly laundered towels to hold myself up.

It sounds as if they are throwing my mother on the floor, taking her by the legs and shaking, the way you would shake out a pillow. I hear thump, thud, and people shouting and rushing from every direction to get into the room.

A nurse rushes out and leads me away into a windowless room. "She'll be okay. They are just trying to revive her," she reassures me. I sit numbly waiting for my mother to reappear. Instead, Dr. Arnstein appears twenty minutes later.

"Your mother is dead." He stand with his hands at his sides.

I don't believe him.

"What happened?"

"I don't know," he says somberly.

"I want to see her."

He leads me back into the x-ray room and leaves me alone there. Behind a closed curtain, she lies on the gray metal table in her patient gown, just as I had seen her minutes ago, alive. Her body still feels warm. I open her closed lids and look carefully into her eyes to get some kind of clue, some last secret message she might have left behind.

I have never noticed the golden specks embedded in the viridian green of her eyes. They are so clear and full of intention. They seem frozen in a moment of recognition. She knew exactly where she was headed when she left, and she didn't seem scared about it.

I run my index finger softly down the length of her left hand. Like a grave robber, I obey her voice inside my head. I pull the rings off her small, thin fingers. "Take these before anyone steals them. They are for you." I quickly follow her orders.

I want her back. Where did she go? Her chest is bony and hard to the touch. My hand rests on her heart until I can no longer bear it. Then I turn, and leave.

18

I pull into the driveway, walk up the path and open the back door. Once inside the house, I can't remember how I got there. In my hand, I carry Mom's shopping bag with the brown flowered muumuu, pink chenille bathrobe, little white sneakers, white-cotton-blend, ankle-length nightgown, pink terrycloth travel slippers, and her small, white summer Gucci handbag.

This house always had a life of its own, at the will and command of my mother. It was a stubborn, stoic, enduring will. Their things still sit on the same shelves and cupboards, or in drawers, but whatever my parents were when they lived here is gone, leaving a vacant space, as if Mom and Dad never inhabited this place.

The plaster of Paris busts of Mozart and Chopin sit on the mantel with the lavender-colored, flowered crystal decanter. They are all cherished possessions of my mother. All the hand-made clay pieces I sculpted in college line the shelves next to the fireplace, with the collection of flowered teacups and saucers meticulously sitting in their miniature wooden holders. My mother and father have withdrawn their spirits from this house, the place they loved and cherished, and now I am sitting with just so many things. Things like at a flea market. Things without an owner to love them and breathe meaning into them.

All my mother's promises to go to Maui with us, to maybe move to California. Were they promises? Or did I want to hear them as promises? I feel betrayed and resentful. Who was this woman, anyway? How could she have hurt me so much? I thought she loved me most of all, but she chose my father in the end.

Dad's menacing presence is gone. I hear a sound. At first it is like a deep growl. Soon it grows louder. I don't recognize my own voice from deep inside my belly howling in pain like a wounded animal lost in a dense thicket. I roam from room to room downstairs, on all fours, searching for my mother.

I propel myself upstairs and yank out all her dresser drawers. The wood hits the headboard of the bed and the floor. I press my nose against her nightgowns, finding her smell. I rush into her closet, flinging her suits and dresses on the bed, searching for some remnant of her. Defeated, I throw myself down the stairs and collapse, sobbing, in the middle of the living room rug.

The portrait of my dad sees me, the ticking clock hears me, the walls stare at me. There is a kind of stillness in the house that is recognizable. Its people have moved away. The emptiness and silence are palpable. I am no one's little girl. I am an orphan. I am a latch-key kid again.

In a strange way, I take pleasure in other people's reactions to my mother's death. As the afternoon drifts away, I enjoy their surprise and then their outpouring of sympathy. I know that I need that sympathy. I leave message after message on answering machines for my mother's friends, relatives, David, Rhonda and Harry.

I find comfort in this, while sitting in her flowered recliner in the den. The insistent hum of the bees hovering around the red, bristly, bottle brush hedge just beneath the window outside, the ticking of the clock on the mantel, the thick heat as the sun presses down on the tar roof of the den, make me drift back to a time when I waited for her to walk up the driveway on the way home from work. I waited just like I've done all my life. I wait for David, Rhonda and Harry to arrive. It is a waiting house. Waiting to grow up, waiting to fall in love, waiting to escape, and now waiting to bury my mother.

I begin calling and making arrangements for the funeral in an efficient, no-nonsense way, like she taught me. The doorbell rings and in a daze, I answer it. It is Rhonda, who brings me a sandwich. I am grateful even though I protest. Later Stella Miller brings lasagna. I open the refrigerator and deep in the back I find some brisket and potatoes, and half a chicken and gravy.

The house is filling up with people. By seven o'clock, Harry, Roberta and Francine are there. David arrives about a half-hour later. The six of us sit together around the dining room table. We congregate awkwardly with each other, silent and stunned. My mother has been the glue, the raconteur, the one who keeps conversation flowing at events like this.

If life had gone as planned, I would have been back in California by now. My plane would have been landing, and Mom would have been back at home, heating up this brisket for herself and pleasantly remembering our visit. Perhaps we would be talking on the phone in an hour.

"Oh, Honey, your visit went so fast. I hardly knew you were here," she would say.

"Mom, I am so proud of you learning how to drive," I would answer.

Any friction or irritations would have been forgotten by now.

I spread a table of her china and silver. Rhonda says softly, "Your mother always set a beautiful table."

In the freezer, I find some chocolate cake and cookies. Underneath these is some frozen apple pie. I defrost these. I put the brisket on the stove under a low flame and warm up with the potatoes.

"Sarah was the best cook," Rhonda says to the guests seated around the table. I notice the past tense. The awkwardness is broken by the strident ring of the kitchen phone.

It is Rabbi Gruen. "I'm returning your call. I'm sorry about your mother. I called to find out what you want me to say at the funeral service," he says in an indifferent voice.

"My God, you've known my mom and dad forty years and you want to know what to say?" I say, angered. "I'll speak. I'll write something. I want it in the big sanctuary," I add, and slam down the phone.

I go back to the dining room table. Shame smothers me for a moment. Then I get my bearings. I am my mother's daughter. They paid good money to belong to that temple, money they couldn't afford, and he didn't even know what to say? It feels good to be angry at someone.

I find a pencil and paper and sit down at the table.

"What do you remember about Mom?" I ask Harry, Rhonda, David and Francine. No one speaks.

"I could tell about her learning to drive," I say.

"Mom had guts," says Harry. I knew that to be true. I write it down under number one on my paper.

Francine tries to smother a giggle. "How about how Grandma always make sure I had on clean underwear before I left the house?" she says. "That way, if I had an accident and landed in the hospital, I wouldn't embarrass the family. They'd know from my underwear that I came from a good family."

Harry smiles. "Leave that one out," he says dryly.

"She was such a good homemaker, a real *balabusta*," Rhonda adds.

We eat in silence. The more I eat, the hungrier and more unnourished I feel. I want to fill up every available space in myself with the sweetness of her now. I get up and walk to the refrigerator while rehearsing the eulogy in my mind.

It takes no time to defrost the pie, cake and cookies because the night air is so warm. Every few minutes, I cut off slivers with a wet knife that I pass under hot water at the sink, then I lick off the excess. I put the apple pie, chocolate cake and cookies onto two separate plates and bring them into the dining room, to pass them around. Dessert lubricates the conversation. Soon we are all remembering, eating and laughing.

Harry says, "I always tried to clean up the house when she came for a visit. But she always found where I stashed all the dirty stuff, and started washing it for me."

David remembers the time Mom made him his favorite cake, and by evening, he had eaten the whole thing. "She always laughed at my jokes," he says.

This evening the desserts Mom prepared are passed around, and the chunks become slices, and the slices become slivers, until the serving plates are empty. Finally we pass the empty plates around and lick the crumbs with our wet fingers until all is gone.

Through the alchemy of her ingredients, we fill ourselves with my mother, and she passes into us as a visitation. "Give me a big send-off," she would have said laughingly. And we do. By midnight, we are all high on her stories, and we are ready for the funeral.

Had my mother choreographed the whole thing? She had prepared our last meal for us. With the eating of the food made by her own hands, mixed and spread, we each took in a piece of her for the last time.

That night, I insist that David and I sleep in my parents' bed. I want a sign from Mom. I want to meet her in my dreams.

She is somewhere close, and I am going to find her. That night, I sleep in her place in their bed, but I have no dreams.

The next morning, Harry greets me at breakfast. "You must pay me to go through Mom's estate."

"How much?" I am shocked at this callous demand after the closeness of the evening before.

"My rate is two hundred dollars an hour," he says.

"How long do you think it will take?" I want to know what he is thinking.

"About two months, more or less," he says.

"I'd be happy to discuss this after the funeral," I say while I calculate the numbers in my mind.

All day I ruminate and rage at this demand. It is hard to separate the brother I knew growing up from the brother who is with me now. Is Mom's warning coming true, that Harry will take all her money and leave nothing in return?

The first thing I do when my brother is out of sight is to call my mother's lawyer. I set up an appointment to discuss the estate with him and my brother at his office the day after the funeral.

The next day, we bury her in her new beige-and-white flowered silk skirt with her linen jacket over a silk shell she bought for her Maui trip. I know I should have buried her in that white boxy, poly-blend dress with gold buttons and short sleeves. It was the dress she had planned to wear to New York with me for my interview. The last I remember, it was hanging ready to wear on the outside of her bedroom door. And then she is gone. I am struck by the stillness of the setting, under that tree in a cemetery that is surrounded by factories. Only the sound of the dirt hitting the lid of the wooden box as the grave is covered, strikes deep into my heart. The incongruity of it all: my mother's soft body, the soft silk skirt, a wooden box in the ground and dirt.

That dress is the only piece of her clothing that I take back to California with me-not her pink chenille robe, not her brown Maui Hilo Hattie muumuu, not her three fancy suits that she bought at Miss Lillian's in Millburn.

So that humid twenty-first day of June in 1993 when we lower her into the ground next to my dad under the shade tree in Kenilworth, New Jersey, I can hear them laughing, that although they are not the richest couple in the cemetery, they certainly are the best-dressed.

I wish I had a quiet moment to hear my mother and what she wants to tell me, but I am too angry at my brother and Rabbi Gruen to hear anyone.

"Harry, how long do you think it will take you to dispose of your family's estate?" Mr. Feinstein asks.

Harry leaves a long pause, then answers Mr. Feinstein's question. "About a month."

"Harry, that could cost your sister close to thirty-two thousand dollars. Do you know what you are asking? Don't you and your sister have the same goal — to dispose of the items and sell the house? I think it's a very inappropriate request to ask her to pay you at all," says Mr. Feinstein.

Harry imperceptibly shifts in his seat. When he speaks next, his voice is soft and wavering. "I'm just afraid that she will fly back to California and leave me to clean everything up." His eyes moisten.

I feel an old shame well up inside my gut about earlier years, when I was seen by my family as irresponsible and unpredictable: a longhaired hippie, wearing sandals and living in Berkeley. I feel my heart open — like grass sprouting up between cracks in a cement sidewalk.

"I'll stay to help you," I respond. I want Harry to know that I wasn't that other person the family typecast me as before.

So that week Harry and I work side by side trying to sort through the contents of the house. It is tiring work.

The days grow hotter, and by late afternoon I'm exhausted, but grief, anxiety and the lump in my gut drive me to complete this task. I don't want to disappoint my brother.

When the sun goes down and the sound of crickets and the lights of fireflies appear, we barely talk to each other. Our grief imprisons our hearts.

At night I lie in my parents' bed on my mother's side quietly sobbing, resenting that confusing silence. My brother is on the other side of the wall, in his room. At night, somehow, he turns into the enemy again. Who is this grown man who has betrayed me? I lock the door at night, not so much for my grown self, but for the smaller, younger one who is still wounded from that girlhood experience.

Each day I go through my mother's things, for Harry seems focused on Dad's. I look for a letter slipped between her nightgowns, or a folded sheet of paper addressed to me and me alone. It will explain what has happened.

"My dear," it would say. "I loved you the best of all. I am sorry I disappointed you by dying. I really wanted to spend the rest of my life with you and David, and live with you. But Dad needed me."

What kind of life would that have been for her? Maybe it was a blessing that she went quickly. Would I have had to resuscitate her in my home if she had had a heart attack? Would she have died alone three thousand miles away from her home, in a strange nursing home?

I look under the white paper in which she lined her drawers but I find nothing. No messages, no secrets, only vast hours of space and papers and clothes and jewelry and pots and pans and dishes. She has given me no space — not an inch — when she was alive. She was always in my face. Now there is nothing but space.

That night I dream that my mother comes to me in her pink bathrobe: she seems to appear from inside the closet. My father hangs back behind her. I beg her to take me with her. I sob so hard that I am gasping for breath. "No, Dear, life is for the living. You must stay here. You have a long, happy life ahead of you."

She shows me through wordless pictures what will happen if I follow her. Afterlife is like a large garment, but the seam is on the other side. If I find out how to leave, I may never get back. I understand it then, and I let them go. Sad and miserable, I lie awake until morning, lulled by the insomniac sound of some chirping night birds.

In the middle of the week, I am in the attic going through her things when I come across a suitcase that has a combination lock on it. I ask my mother for the combination, and I hear her say, "It's Dad's birthday, Honey." I set the rollers on 6-06-10, and the lock snaps open for me. Inside I find some old love letters from Dad to her, and a postcard from another man. It is dated 1936. It must have been during her nurse's training. He scribbled, "I want to get to know you. I'm a friend of Ann's, your roommate. I was watching you in the cafeteria the other day. Love, Jake."

Did my mom save this because she was flattered by his attention? And what of the other love letters? They crinkle to the touch, as if they will break if I handle them too roughly. Each is filled with idealistic platitudes. Hallmark cards with love poems from Dad. Years of birthdays, anniversaries celebrated together. I feel cheated that Dad used store-bought sentiments.

I sit in the attic all afternoon, until I can feel the sun going down on the side of the house and hear my brother call me from downstairs. In the den, Harry stacks the books that Dad treasured in neat little piles on the green carpet. He holds a frayed letter in his hand. "I found this in one of Dad's books." He hands it to me.

On a half-sheet of discolored writing paper, a letter was penned in careful script. In the upper right-hand corner is the date — June 12, 1929. It was signed by a Mr. Litman, Law Professor at Rutgers University. It appears to be an answer to a query that my dad has sent to a man he didn't know about how to become a lawyer.

It seems to me that Dad's letter must have been very naïve. I can tell by how Mr. Litman wrote back to him — a rather arrogant and pompous note as to how one achieves success. I only hoped that Dad was not put off.

That day I find another letter, too. It is in the bottom drawer of his dresser, under the white-shelf paper. It is about twenty pages, and it goes on and on about how someone is trying to get him fired. It must have been when Dad had his nervous breakdown, and was trying sort things out in his mind about what was real and what was his paranoia. It is the only thing I have ever seen where my dad expresses his real feelings in writing. I understand that I haven't given him much credit for having big dreams or for being sensitive.

That night as we are sitting in the den watching television, Harry begins to talk to me in a way I have never heard before. "I've got to get back home. If I don't, I'm afraid that Roberta will do something crazy."

"What?" I ask, dumbfounded.

"If I'm gone for a while, I'm not sure what I'll find when I get back," he says.

"What do you mean?" I still am not following this sudden outburst of intimacy.

"Well, one time I found her in the closed garage, with the car running."

"Oh, my God," I gasp. "Did Mom and Dad know about this?"

"I don't think so," he says.

"What do you mean, you don't think so?"

"Well, I think Mom guessed it."

We go on, watching the television and sitting without speaking. I am trying to make sense of what he has just told me. I feel the solidity of his body, like a bull, staying the course, even when it is destructive. Like my Dad — one marriage, one woman, one job, and you are set for life. For a moment I hover between emotions. Finally, I settle on a deep sadness about this part of his life that I have never known before.

I move closer and put my hand on his arm. His eyes are moist and so are mine. We sit like this for a while.

19

When I return to California, my grief manifests itself in searching, forgetfulness and fear. I urge David to put a burglar alarm in the house. I buy a car alarm and bring my cats permanently indoors. I hide my jewelry so no one can steal it. When David is working in Fremont and stays overnight, I drown my fears in glasses of wine.

I am obsessed with the fact that my mother died of an embolism, that's what Dr. Arnstein said over the phone. He reassured me that they did all they could. He even suggested an autopsy if I had doubts. But I know that my dad took her and they are dancing under the trees near their burial site.

That night I dream that Dad comes to my bedside with a gift. In his opened palms there is a tiny white kitten, its blue eyes looking up at me. He remembered! He must be okay on the other side!

Then I have another dream. I dream that I have murdered someone: not Mom, Dad, Harry or David. I can't remember where I put the body. The thought of this secret terrorizes me in the stark, quiet night.

I sit in the big white easy chair in the living room at 3 a.m. reflecting on these dreams. What seems to be emerging lately is the fragile little girl from my childhood, the one underneath the one my mother bullied into becoming strong and self-reliant — this ancient, sweet child wants to become reacquainted with me. She wants to express herself creatively in ways that have been intimidated out of her. Perhaps I have murdered this child, but I want to find her body in my psyche and resurrect her. I go out into the garden with colored chalks, and in swift crazy abandon, I begin drawing huge pastel pictures of my family on the walls and sidewalks around my house. I run wild, until I collapse in tears of laughter and exhaustion. Now that my cloying mother is dead, I feel a certain relief to become the self I never felt I could become before.

On one hand I am overcome with a sense of freedom. This half-century of an ancient umbilical cord which stretched three thousand miles, has snapped, and now, I have an enormous amount of mental and physical energy that I haven't had in decades. On the other hand, a picture of every hour and minute of the last few months are burned into my memory. I will be haunted by them. Above all, there is a hole in my middle deeper and darker than anything I could have imagined. There are even times when I'd give anything just to relive the last few minutes with Mom and Dad, no matter how awful they were, because even the worst moments are better than knowing there will never be any more.

Yet, I am truly free. I can make up a new name. I can divorce my husband, or better, I can just disappear one day and never come back. I can become some new person with a new identity in Morocco, or the Amazonian rain forest, or Moscow. I am no one's daughter. But try as I might to plan my escape to assuage my grief, as in my escape fantasies of my childhood, my imagination will not come to my aid. If I first mastered marriage to prove something to my mother, now I have invested too much in my relationship with David over the years, and loved too deeply, to run. I stay put. Softly and slowly, this marriage has truly become mine to cherish.

One morning, when I've been home for several days, the phone rings. It is Harry in Maryland. He is sobbing.

"Roberta hung herself."

"What?" I couldn't take it in at first. "How did it happen?"

"I came home and had to cut her down from the landing. She found some rope I used for my computer boxes in the basement. She must have jumped over the railing, because she landed in the dining room. She was all purple and black. She looked so awful. Oh, I had to cut her down." He sobs again. "The police and the medical examiners are here now. Please come. I haven't told Francine yet."

Before I leave, David and I spend many hours late into the night talking about what made her take her life.

"Living a life is an awesome task. How thin the membrane between order and chaos," he says.

Despite a loyal husband, a vital, life-giving daughter, a community of caring and thoughtful friends, Roberta felt alone, isolated and alienated.

As I board the plane once again, this time to Washington Dulles, I never thought that I would be going on a trip to my sister-in-law's funeral. Life is unfolding so strangely. Sometimes the things I worry about never happen, and the things that never cross my mind cross my path. Maybe I'm not worrying as comprehensively as I could. Since the shocking news, I feel like I am watching a miniseries on television. This is someone else's life, not mine.

I know that Roberta died of shame. She was ashamed that she had to leave school a month earlier because she couldn't cope with her inner demons, and she was ashamed to talk about it. She died of shame because she couldn't make sense out of what was happening. She thought she had her illness of seventeen years ago licked, but it came back and terrorized her. She died of shame because she was overwhelmed and couldn't find the words, or the safety in herself, to talk about her inner landscape with others as deeply and as honestly or as fully as she was experiencing it.

I knew in myself that under the right confluence of circumstances this panic, this terror, resided close by, inside me, as well.

On the plane I think about how the first half of my life was about acquisition — acquiring a degree from college, finding a career, getting married. This second half truly is about divestment: parents dying, loss of vitality and aging. Saying goodbye to my pictures of reality. Maybe David is right, I think as we fly toward Dulles and I look down at the green rolling hills of Virginia, it is a daunting task facing one's inner landscape in the second half of one's life. "Menopause can kill you," Roberta once told to me. I hadn't believed her then, but I do now.

I have a strange respect for her as we land. Courageously, Roberta has done the best she could, but ultimately, perhaps in a moment of panic, the terror took over, she couldn't find the strength to tame her darkness.

I thought about my parting from David at the airport. He had spent the morning on the phone trying to correct a mistake on his Visa credit card. His frustration was palpable, because the woman helping him had a Russian accent and kept calling his card a "wisa." I thought we'd be late for the plane and my irritation was visible as we arrived at the departure gate.

"I wish I could give you something to take to keep you safe and remember me by. It may be rough going back there," he said lovingly.

"How about your 'wisa?'" I joked.

When I arrive at Harry's house, Francine opens the door. She looks shell-shocked and withdrawn. I grab her to hug her, but she draws back, crying.

I hug my brother. His body is hard and dense, like a bear's.

"Did she leave a note?" I ask.

"I haven't found anything," he says.

While Harry is calling relatives, talking to the rabbi and making funeral arrangements, I go into the kitchen to make supper, but the kitchen cabinets are a mess and I quickly give up. I go upstairs to put my suitcase in Roberta's study. Each room is in various states of chaos. I take large piles of washed and unwashed clothes off the bed to make room for myself.

Francine comes in and watches me. "You didn't like my mother much, did you?" she says. She stares at me angrily. I am taken back by her clarity, but I opt for some form of the truth. How can a fifteen-year-old understand the complexity of the relationship I had with her mother?

"Your mother and I were very different people. I didn't always understand her, but I liked her all right. Sometimes she did things that annoyed me," I concede.

There is a long silence. "I overheard Mom and Dad talking the day that Grandpa died. Mom told Dad that you didn't like her."

"Sometime when people die, it releases a lot of energy. I said that in anger and she said things in anger that we were both sorry for later."

"Sometimes I felt like I didn't like her either," Francine says, and stands there silently.

I put my arms around her and we sit on the bed in grief. I am overcome with sadness and love for this girl I really don't know very well. We have never spent much time together, and she is a mirror of her mother in many ways: her long, dark hair and her Semitic nose, her short, stocky body. Yet, this young stranger is the last remaining legacy of the Perlmans. In my will I have named her, after my husband, to dispose of all my possessions and inherit all my things. I know so little about her because her mother always kept me from her, but now there is an opening for some connection.

"It is okay not to like your mom sometimes. I didn't like my mom all the time. Ask Harry. We had these yelling matches and then we made up. How else can you unfold, like a seedling, pushing up from the soil, if you don't have a mom to push up against, to grow into your own person, how are you supposed to do it? That is one part of what moms are for," I say. I want to give her all my wisdom born out of the pain I have endured over the last half-century.

She huddles in herself, on the bed, with her hands around her knees and her head tucked into her chest, thoughtful and confused.

I can't sleep at Harry's place that night. I wander from room to room. Everywhere I go, it feels like Roberta's energy has vacated the spaces a long time ago. Yet, each room has a eerie quality of someone ransacking the place, leaving it disheveled, turning things upside down, as if to find something important. What was she looking for so unsuccessfully?

Unsettled after the long flight and this shocking news, I sit in the living room surrounded by her garish taste of bright yellow walls and orange upholstered furniture. I am afraid to sit in the family room because I think that Roberta's ghost resides there. I don't want to touch the railing or feel Roberta's vibes.

Harry paints an image of Roberta when he cut her down. "She was contorted, blue, like Lurch," he says. "If she knew how she looked, she wouldn't have hung herself."

Earlier, Harry really unloaded on me, the years of pain. He said that for several weeks before, she didn't want to be hugged, kissed or touched. She told him he needed to learn to be on his own. "I didn't understand what that meant at the time," he said. "She must have been planning this all along."

It is dusk when we return from the funeral, and fireflies in the backyard flicker in the night sky. They remind me of my girlhood in Maplewood, when we collected them in jam jars, puncturing the lids with holes so they could breathe. Francine and I stand in the darkened backyard trying to capture some in our hands. "You know, we don't have these out in California. I had forgotten about them, but now I really miss them," I say to her.

Francine is about the same age that I was when the incident happened with Harry's friends. The thought makes me shiver inside. I wonder if he ever learned of it. I wonder if he recognizes that Francine is a nubile girl around my age when his friends came after me.

Early on in my relationship with David, he first met Harry over dinner and asked him about our childhood. David wanted to know what kind of kid I was in Harry's eyes. Harry was short and swift with reproach. "I don't want to talk about it. The difference between being adults and children is that you can control your life." His tone stopped David short of pursing further conversation.

I go inside and find Harry lying on their king-sized bed. I sit down across from him. "I can't get the image out of my head of cutting her down. If she could have seen herself, she never would have done it. She was so concerned with how she looked." He is crying.

I sit with him in silence. There is nothing to say. Could I ask him about that long-ago episode now, or would that just rub salt in his wound? My mother was like that, kicking you when you were down. I hated that about her, but I know that I have an inclination to do the same thing. No, now is not the right time, I decide.

He speaks first. "As I get older, I love the liturgy in temple." He picks up the prayer book and begins reading a psalm to me.

Then I read him a passage of something that I have come across during the silent prayer in temple. He closes his eyes to listen. I feel so grateful for this moment after such a long season of bitterness towards him.

Later we go down into the basement, and he shows me his new computer and scanner. There we find Francine with her dog, Ruffer. I show her how to make her dog sleepy by hypnotizing him and rubbing his eyelids shut, like a charlatan performer. She begins to laugh with me as Ruffer jumps off her lap and runs upstairs.

By week's end, the days begin to feel long and endless. The house becomes crammed and cluttered with food and streams of people paying their respects. It is getting to me. I am losing it. I feel like I am wearing the wrong clothes, looking wrong. I feel crowded and crammed in my body. We walk to temple yet another time, and Francine says to me, "You don't fit in here."

I try to remain calm. "Why do you say that?" I ask casually.

"You are so laid-back, like my California classmates."

"She doesn't dye her hair," my brother adds.

"Oh that, it shows a lot of confidence," Francine says.

After years of trying to understand what they think of me, pieces of impressions are slipping out gradually.

As friends and guests pay their respects, I look at the railing Roberta climbed over, several yards away from where people are eating their casseroles at the dining room table. They don't know that she was dangling, a dead weight, right in front of them not more than seventy-two hours ago.

After several days, panic that I won't be able to find my way home again sets in. I am beginning to feel Harry's neediness, and the horror of Roberta's death is seeping in. The mess around me that felt like an oddity at first is getting to me.

Roberta's friends come to express their condolences. They seem so much older than me, even though I am chronologically older. I find myself sitting with them in traditional Jewish *Shiva*, mourning behavior, but I really want to be with Francine and her teenage friends in the family room. I hate making small talk about the cost of time-shares in Palm Beach. I hate how I pick on my cuticles until my fingers ache. I hate how frightened I am of my feelings, and I try to act strong and tough it out through the hard parts of these endless days.

I am awakened one morning by Harry, wanting us to go downstairs for a *minion* of prayers. Like a group of insomniacs, Roberta's friends are here again praying in Hebrew. Only twenty minutes, Harry says, but it is goes on for an hour and a half. I opt out after grabbing a cup of coffee and a hard, stale bagel. I find refuge upstairs in Francine's bedroom on the mattress on the floor. The life of the "shoulds" is what killed Roberta.

I find my peace quietly reading until the *dovening* circle, the Jewish Olympics of prayers and chanting is over. *Kayn ayn hore*, warding off evil, didn't help Roberta! No one broke through and said, "Talk to me, I'm coming over and staying until you talk it out."

When I finally return to Mill Valley, I am a mess. David picks me up from the airport. "I wouldn't put it past my brother to help her kill herself," I say to him in exasperation and relief that I finally made it home safely. "He probably gave her the rope."

"You have quite an imagination," he says laughingly. "Sure, he may look like an ax murderer with the beard and all, but he wouldn't hurt a flea."

"Don't count on it!" I reply.

"Why would you say something like that?" He looks at me long and hard, with a critical expression in his eyes.

"Remember the time when Ted Kaczynski, the Unabomber, was caught? Harry and I were discussing it over the phone, and he said to me, if that ever happened to me, would you turn me in? At first we were joking, but it turned serious. Remember, I told you. 'In a heartbeat,' I responded. He understood that we could joke and be close, but in the end I still held a wariness and distrust of him."

"But why?" asks David. "I can't understand that about you and him. He's just a quiet guy. You mistake quiet for sinister."

"Because of something I've never told you about myself," I say cautiously. I walked right into this. I feel caught now. A part of me wants to tell him, and a part wants to slip out the back door.

"What? I thought after all these years I knew everything." He puts his arm around me.

"My brother betrayed me."

David takes his foot off the gas and slowly lets the car glide to a stop on a side street along 19th Avenue. He turns toward me.

It is then that I tell him everything that happened in the house that day, long ago. His face softens and he pulls me toward him, and in the franticness of the rush of cars outside, we are in the eye of stillness as we hug and kiss.

"I can never forgive him!" I say, with tears running down my face. I look into David's blue steady gaze. "But the more

I am around Harry, I can't help but feel a softening and a healing. You can't imagine what a horrible wound I have carried around all these years; it has warped my emotions towards all men, even you at times."

"Why haven't you ever told me?" he asks.

"I've been so ashamed that I let it happen. I blamed myself."

"Your mother died not ever knowing?"

"I think she might have suspected something. She was no one's fool."

"Did you ever confront your brother?"

"No, I just couldn't. I don't think there would be any use. But I do know that it was your love that helped me forgive my brother and my father's ineptness."

He puts his arms around me, and I feel a safety net under me. I can endure anything with this loving man by my side. In that moment, I know that out of all the craziness and unconsciousness that life dealt me, I have found safety and trust in this man. Together we have carved out a life of our own three thousand miles away. I know he loves me with fierceness and loyalty burning in his heart, and his love fills all the hurt places of the past. Nothing can destroy that. For this I am forever grateful.

I think of how my old girlhood hurt is like the breast cancer that has left a scar. Even though the surgeon had promised it would heal, it hadn't. In trying to heal, it became keloid, raw and red. It covered itself over with a bigger lump of redness. I was embarrassed to undress in front of David, because I knew that the scar was unsightly under my clothes. But years later I glanced at it as I was undressing in a locker room before swimming. The scar had all but disappeared. What had been hard, dense tissue had turned into a faint line, almost like the laugh lines around my eyes. I touched it and felt how delicate and fine it had become. I actually grew to like it there, because it was mine, and it reminded me of a time I had endured and survived. Through my tears today, I realize that is how it is with Harry. In the process of making a life with David, I let go of this wound slowly, and unnoticed, it has vanished. I can let go of Harry now. My life has become my own.

The End

Acknowledgments

A book is never written alone. It was written with the love and support of many people.

This is for Ron who has given me inspiration, love and compassion.

This is for Elsa Hurley, Cyra McFadden, Jean McMann and the writing group, Lyn Follett and Abby Wasserman who have made me work hard and be smarter.

This is for Erica Ross Kreiger who kept me going.

This is for Susan Campbell, Miriam Licht, Gilda Meyers, Annie Styron Leonard, Kent Black, Kate Lynch, David Hayward, Jeff Anderson, Sharon Norman, Nixy Rickles and Fu Schroeder and the Friday morning meditation group whose love and kindness were central to this book.

This is for Walter and Naomi Hillinger, Amber and John Bremmer, Jean Parr, Fulton Toshombe, Alana and Don Gilmore, and my Maui friends, who listened to my dreams.

This is for Larry and Barbara Brauer whose exception caring and patience helped me through.

This is for Toni Littlejohn and The Wild Carrots Art Group, Peter Horvath and my friends at Sight and Insight Art Center who permitted me to soar.

www.ingramcontent.com/pod-product-compliance
Lightning Source LLC
Chambersburg PA
CBHW022007050726
47499CB00003BA/745

9 780974 692753